LOVE IS A TEMPEST

*Also by Angela Gordon
in Large Print:*

A Game Called Love
Love In Her Life

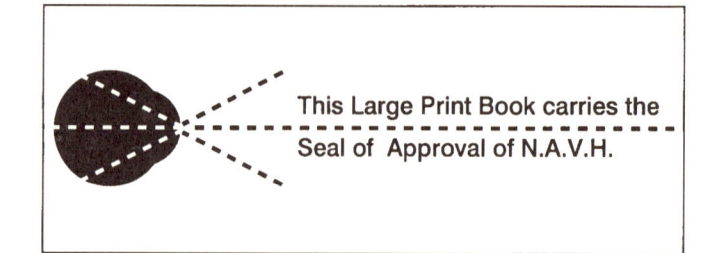

This Large Print Book carries the Seal of Approval of N.A.V.H.

LOVE IS A TEMPEST

ANGELA GORDON

G.K. Hall & Co.
Thorndike, Maine

Copyright © Robert Hale Limited 1969

All rights reserved.

Published in 1997 by arrangement with
Golden West Literary Agency.

G.K. Hall Large Print Paperback Collection.

The text of this Large Print edition is unabridged.
Other aspects of the book may vary from the original edition.

Set in 16 pt. Plantin by Al Chase.

Printed in the United States on permanent paper.

Library of Congress Cataloging in Publication Data
Gordon, Angela, 1916–
   Love is a tempest / Angela Gordon.
     p. cm.
   ISBN 0-7838-8317-X   (lg. print : sc : alk. paper)
   1. Large type books.   I. Title.
[PS3566.A34L69   1997]
   813'.54—dc21   97-36288

CONTENTS

1	A Not-So-Quiet Rebellion	7
2	The Day Ends	15
3	A Time Of Trial	25
4	Meetings And Adjustments	35
5	Different Kinds Of Men	44
6	Under A Troubled Moon	54
7	The Spontaneous Conspiracy	64
8	A Secret Is No Longer A Secret	74
9	The Blow Falls!	83
10	The Storm And Tumult	93
11	The Crises Anew	103
12	Playing A Part?	113
13	An Ungentlemanly Act	123
14	The Aftermath Of Unpleasantness	133
15	A Clanger!	143
16	"Goodbye, Arthur"	152
17	It Isn't Ended	162
18	Different Attitudes	172
19	An Evening At Home	181
20	An End To Memory	191
21	Grandfather Morris Speaks	201
22	"Because There Are No Islands"	211

CHAPTER ONE

A NOT-SO-QUIET REBELLION

It made no difference to Grandfather Morris that Arthur Cartier had inherited fifty thousand dollars from a vague and distant relative. "An actor," he had said more than once, "is, by the very nature of his calling, unstable."

No one disputed this, not necessarily because no other members of the clan were sufficiently knowledgeable to do so, but primarily because no one disputed Grandfather Morris.

There was another reason, too. With the exception of Grandfather Morris's daughter's husband, thickset and decidedly plebeian George Jarrett, all the others were reverential towards age. Especially since age, in this instance, was worth upwards of five million dollars, and because age — in this instance being past seventy — was going to prove immortal.

George, sitting with cigar clamped in teeth, put everyone on edge by glaring at the old man across the great baronial hall and saying, "Mister Morris, an actor named Booth shot President Lincoln a hundred years ago, and since that time we've had plenty of statesmen including Presidents shot, and not a single damned other actor was involved."

George Jarrett obdurately refused to call his father-in-law by the patriarchal title of Grandfather. He was the only hold-out, and to the dolorous resignation of his wife, he showed no signs of weakening in this regard even after twenty years in the family.

Grandfather Morris glared back. "They don't have to shoot Presidents, drat it, George. They are scatter-brains, opportunistic activists for all the harebrained schemes that crop up, and I defy you to point out one — just *one* — that has been a moral person. Just *one!*"

George reached, wrenched out his cigar and said, "Jesus!"

The shock was so great that no one moved, spoke, or even seemed to breathe for the space of five seconds. By then George was ready.

"He stood before multitudes preaching, Mister Morris. He out-did Houdini with miracles. He was not only an actor, sir, He was a fantastically *good* one. Two thousand years and oceans of blood later, people still revere His name."

Grandfather Morris, millionaire merchant, iron-hearted — and headed, if one believed all the tales — internationalist, was scarcely the devout type, and yet he could not stomach this, so he struck the oak table beside his chair and said, "George, you are a nincompoop! I warn you for the last time, if you permit Heloise to marry *that actor*, I'll. . . ."

Jarrett was on his feet, hands clenched, thick jaw out-thrust, bleak little pale eyes flashing cold fire. "You'll do what? Let *me* tell *you* something, *Mister* Morris. For damned near a quarter of a century I've bit my tongue for Alice's sake. I've watched you browbeat everyone in this room, dominate their lives, ruin some, spoil others, and I've never allowed you to interfere with my family, and *I'll see you in hell before I'll permit it now!*"

Alice Jarrett said softly, "Please, George . . ." and twisted the tiny shred of lace handkerchief to bits in her fingertips. She was pale and distraught. In a way she resembled her father, except that the chin was rounder, softer, more sensual, and the mouth was heavier and weaker. She had made a good wife for George Jarrett and a good mother to Heloise, their daughter, but being the only surviving daughter of Grandfather Morris may have been a source of anguish to the old man because she had inherited none of his iron.

On the other hand, it was hard to imagine George Jarrett, who had enough iron for them both, staying married to an iron-willed Morris for twenty years, so perhaps it was as well Alice was not gifted with the old-time Morris spirit.

Grandfather Morris leaned in his chair. He was old and there were annoying infirmities — which he scorned as personal enemies — but they had not dampened any of the fierce Morris spirit. "And what would you say," he rapped out, "if I were to tell you that neither you *nor* Heloise will inherit a red cent from me if she marries this — this *actor!*"

George had expected this, had in fact been

waiting all evening for it, had scarcely touched the formal supper because he was geared for fighting not fraternising, and now he slowly smiled a very wicked smile and said, raising a clenched fist towards the old man. "You had your say when we named her. Heloise, for your grandmother, which is one hell of a name for *anyone*. You got your way when Alice and I started out — putting me up in the company empire as a kind of backsteps, honorary Morris. You had your way when we decided which schools to send our daughter to, but, by God, tonight it ends. I'll tell you what you can do with your five million dollars. . . ."

"Steady, George," said grey and thin-lipped Carleton Morris, Alice's only brother and Grandfather Morris's only surviving son. "Careful of the language."

George swung. "Carleton, I've wanted to knock your teeth out for twenty years. If you leave that chair I'll do it now, s'help me!" He faced Grandfather Morris again, white and fierce and obviously capable of doing most of what he said he'd do. "Take your lousy five million, *Mister* Morris, and divide it up among the parasites you see in this room with you tonight. They're only waiting for you to die to roll up both sleeves and bury their puny arms in the loot anyway. But don't you dare leave a stinking dime of your filthy money to me or mine! Alice, go and get your coat."

Carleton gripped both arms of his chair, glaring. George turned on him very slowly, and smiled. "All right," he said. "You want to salvage the Morris honour; get up out of that chair!"

Grandfather Morris's voice was thin, reedy, as he gave a curt order. "Carleton, stay exactly where you are. All of you, stay where you are."

They sat like stricken children while the brimstone scent of near-violence filled the huge old hall. The only sound was made by Alice, returning with her coat, handbag and gloves. She looked like a ghost as she stopped near her husband of twenty years, her dark eyes huge and hurt. Then she floated past towards the flagstoned entry-hall and they could very distinctly make out the soft closing of the huge front door.

George loosened slightly, checked the hang of his dinner-jacket with both big hands, glowered, then turned on his heel and also walked out.

For as long as it took the Jarretts to get into their car, start the motor and drive slowly down the winding private roadway to the city street, no one had a word to offer.

But afterwards Carleton, fishing through his dinner-jacket pockets for a cigar, and finding none, turned to his cousin, Michael Morris, and said, "Would you hand me the humidor off that end table, please?"

Michael handed it, then fell to inspecting an invisible hangnail. He was a tallish, pale, black-haired man with lips like a steel trap and eyes like dagger-points. He was never very talkative and tonight he seemed to have quite lost the ability to converse altogether.

Grandfather Morris sought for a means to patch up the evening, and since business was all he knew it was perhaps to be expected that he turned to that now, speaking as though there hadn't just occurred a rupture in the family the like of which no one had ever seen, or even heard of, before.

"Carleton, what has been done towards arranging for the disposal of that Maine tract of land?"

"Nothing really, Father. I went up there last week, as you know, and the amount of development inclines me to believe it should not be sold at this time."

Grandfather Morris's eyes fastened on his son's face. "Sell it. I thought you knew better than to be one of those idiots who believe because something is of value to someone else, it must therefore also be of value to its owner. We are not land-developers. We deal in commodities and in cash. Sell the land."

"Yes," murmured Carleton, and retreated ignominiously behind the cloud of fragrant smoke.

"Michael!"

The son of Grandfather Morris's long-dead brother sat a little straighter. "Yes sir."

"Tell me again about the bankruptcy proceedings down at Portsmouth. The others would like to hear it, too."

The women tried to look alert, the men attentive, as Michael Morris said, "It's a very old firm, sir. Started out over a hundred years ago as a chandler's establishment; gradually got into shipbuilding, outfitting, and for the past two generations into wholesale hardware. The owner passed on two years ago. Since then a stepson has let the business go to ruin. They filed for bankruptcy last month. I got hold of a copy of the inventory, had it audited for worth, and including land and buildings, the bankruptcy should just about clear indebtedness."

"And why would we want such an establishment, Michael?"

"Sir, it has a great potential, both as a seaside commercial hardware business, and also as a base for importing and exporting."

Grandfather Morris nodded. "And it can be acquired cheaply," he said, sounding like an old schoolmaster prompting a dullard pupil. "Eh?"

"Yes sir. By paying off the debts."

"Very well. And what do we have to pay this wastrel stepson?"

"Nothing," said Michael, studying that elusive hangnail again. "Unless he clears up the debts they'll have a judgement against him; he'll never be able to open another store, nor for the matter of that, own anything in his own name."

"You've already approached him, Michael?"

"Yes. He'll hand over the title for being made solvent with his creditors, sir."

Grandfather Morris smiled. "Well, Carleton, what do you think of that?"

"It sounds good," said the old man's son. "However, I reserve judgement until I've had a close look. Did you have that in mind, Father?"

"I had in mind," said old Morris, pronouncing each word carefully, "having George look into it. But seeing that he'll no longer be participating in *anything* I am concerned with, why then I suppose you may as well make the appraisal, Carleton. Mind you — no shilly-shallying. We give no gratuities. That stepson goes out with his hat and umbrella and not a red cent of my money. Excuse me — *our* money. Right?"

Carleton and Michael nodded in unison. "Right," they said.

CHAPTER TWO

THE DAY ENDS

Alice said, in the privacy of their bedroom, that George had been right. Of course, that put her in the position of taking someone's part in opposition to her father. There was a word for people who did such things. Most places the word was "disloyal," but in New England it was "treason" or "betrayal" for New Englanders had for centuries been both an insular and a clanny people.

"But did you have to shake your fist at him, George, and threaten Carleton? You embarrassed me, you know."

George snorted. "I'd have embarrassed you if I'd simply told your father to go to hell. And maybe I did over-react, Alice, but I've been suppressing my true feelings for twenty years; that ought to be some kind of mitigating circumstance."

Alice loved her husband. She also loved her old father. And of course she loved Ellie — Heloise — her daughter. "All right, George. I'll say no more about it, but it was so abrupt — so — I can't find the exact word, but it left no way back for you."

"Way back? Are you out of your mind, Alice? I *want* no way back." He glared at her, dinner-jacket in hand, curly hair tumbling across his wide forehead.

"Well, but what will you *do,* sweetheart? You've been part of Morris & Morris ever since we've been married."

He flung the dinner-jacket across the foot of their huge double bed as he said, "Dig ditches, trim trees, dung out barns. I'll do whatever I must just to be able to pay the bills, Alice, and every day of it I'll give thanks I got out from under your father's thumb."

She put on a pale, diaphanous dressing gown, sat at her dressing table and began combing her hair. She was quite pretty still, but tonight the reflection gazing back from the mirror had circles under the eyes. "Now it's you that's being melodramatic, George. Of course you won't dig ditches."

"I will!" He stood there without his coat or trousers on, his shirt and tie and gartered socks giving him an undeniably ludicrous appearance for all his irate seriousness. "I'm not being melodramatic at all. If I have to, I'll get a job as a day-labourer."

She looked round at him. "Please, sweetheart, either put your trousers back on, or finish undressing and get into your pyjamas. You don't look like Patrick Henry without your trousers on."

He glared, then stalked loftily to his dressing room, a small closet-like place off the bedroom that one entered before entering the bathroom beyond, and there he growlingly completed the transition from day-time attire to night-time attire. Then he marched back and said, "I wish your brother had got out of that damned chair!"

She was finished with her hair and was now creaming her face. "George, you wouldn't have struck Carleton."

"Wouldn't I have, then?" He laughed in an ugly way from over where he was sliding into bed on his side. "Do you remember, when I was first sparking you, how your brother used to get off those snide remarks if we got home a little late?"

She smiled softly. "I remember. That was just his way. Besides, who cared what he said in those days?"

"I did. But I started holding back right then. It was fatal, Alice. I got into the habit. It's a wonder I didn't develop ulcers over the years. And your brother never stopped making the remarks. He still makes them to this very day. Do you know why?"

"I know your version, George. Because you believe if you'd stopped him 'way-back-when, he wouldn't be making the remarks today."

"And he wouldn't, either!"

Alice finished creaming and went to the bathroom to sponge off the excess grease and brush her teeth. This interrupted their running discourse, but when she returned, George, head propped upon a pillow, beginning to lose some of the truculence that had carried over from his earlier wrath, said, "What a nest of scorpions. Take Cousin Michael; there is one of the most devious, scheming, wholly untrustworthy people I've ever known."

Alice turned to him. "George Jarrett, you have no business making any such statement. What has Michael ever done to you?"

He waggled a finger at her. "He'll never get a chance, I promise you. The man is as slimy as they come. I doubt if he ever had any backbone of his own, but if he did, he sure got rid of it a long while back so the Old Man could run him ragged."

Alice went round to her own side of the bed, climbed in, punched her pillows up and dropped back against them with a soft sigh. "I just wish you hadn't done it — quite that way, George."

He turned towards her. "Alice-love, there is only one way to assert yourself. With conviction and with force."

"You most certainly asserted yourself tonight, then. I doubt if anyone's spoken to my father that way in half a century — if ever. I certainly can't recall it, if it has happened before."

"Look, Alice, I wasn't trying to establish any precedents. I don't care a damn what other people have said to the Old Man, or what they've thought of him. I only care what *I* say and think — and you and Ellie say and think. You see what I'm driving at? We're a family unit, one and indivisible; if we decide to do something as a family, or as individual members of the *Jarrett* family — not the *Morris* family — that's the way it'll be done." He dropped back again, facing the far wall, his breathing slightly heightened and irregular.

She turned cautiously and studied his craggy profile. He'd always been a stubborn, very strong man, and she'd always known some day he'd explode in open rebellion. Perhaps that was what made her feel beneath the covers for his hand now, and squeeze it.

"All right, love," she said. "It's done. I thought I'd drop through the floor when it happened, but now it's done."

"And whether you agree with my method or not, you *do* agree with my reasons?"

"Yes, George."

She made that statement simply and without reservations. What made this possible was the other facet of it — her long-standing knowledge that some day he'd explode. She had spent a number of anguished hours debating her stance when the time eventually arrived. At least she was fortunate in this respect because some women have no warning. But she'd known it would come for many years, and she'd been able to make up her mind slowly about what her position should be. At first she'd thought she might be able to play the part of conciliator. But it didn't take much reflection to realise this was not to be; her father and her husband were too much alike in their wrath to be reconciled by anyone.

So, that left her with a basic choice to make. She'd made it years ago, and tonight she'd had to implement it. She had become a Jarrett something like twenty years ago, and hadn't been a Morris ever since, so her loyalties were those of a Jarrett, unpleasant though that made her feel, particularly this night.

She thought that perhaps she should be grateful they'd had all those serene years. At least outwardly serene years, even though she'd known they hadn't been serene for him.

"Father has his ways, George," she murmured, lying back. "When you're his age you will have, too."

"Not *his* ways I won't!"

"And quite apart," she went on, "from Father's objections to Arthur Cartier, what do you and I know about him, beyond what Ellie told us? He's an actor. He has enormous talent." Alice smiled wanly. "He *is* handsome, of course. One hardly expects an actor to be otherwise."

"Harry Laughton?" he put in. "Lugosi, Tone?"

"George, you're only arguing now for argument's sake."

That was true; as the embers burnt out he still felt an urge for desultory combat. He said, "All right, Arthur's handsome, and all actors are supposed to be that way. And we don't know much about him. I'll make a point to find out more tomorrow. It seems to me, Alice, that if Ellie's old enough to want to marry a man, she's also old enough to make up her own mind. In other words, love, suppose we discover Arthur Cartier is a first-class phony?"

He waited for her answer a long time. Not that he'd caught his wife unprepared, quite the contrary; she was convinced in her secret heart that Arthur Cartier *was* a phony. That's what caused her to raise a hand to her throat now and lie there motionless and silent for so long he had to turn and say, "Well . . . ?" before she answered.

"Then I suppose she will marry him anyway, George, and that will be her tragedy, won't it?"

He leaned to scrutinise his wife's face. "Alice . . . ?"

She turned away, reached for the bed-lamp switch, and plunged their large bedroom into darkness. "Good night, George. I'm tired. It's been a very long evening, hasn't it?"

He said, "Sure. Good night, love," and punched his pillow flat, dropped his head down, closed his eyes, and within moments was snoring softly.

Beyond the open window a great yellow moon rode down the timeless wastes of endless eternity, a bob-tailed owl cut across it moving swiftly in soundless flight, and somewhere across town a train called mournfully into the night to be answered at once by several nearby wailing dogs.

There was little traffic after eleven o'clock any night but Saturday, for Windsor was one of those staid New England towns without industry to draw the dissident groups, where the customs and ethics of earlier generations still largely prevailed.

In front of the Jarrett place left over from those earlier times, stood a thick cast-iron horse's head with a big iron ring in its mouth. The ring was smooth from having held so many horse-tethers over the centuries, although now it stood there all but forgotten, quaint and brown-etched with age. When the low-slung maroon sports car stopped within arm's reach of the tether-post, a very handsome young man, tall and firm and curly-headed, stretched forth to rub the horse's iron muzzle and laugh.

"My good luck charm," he explained to the girl sitting beside him. "The day I don't rub his nose, y'see, there will be a great calamity."

She wrinkled a pert nose. "Such as? The moon will perhaps drop from the sky, Arthur?"

"Oh, much worse, Ellie, much worse." He thought a moment, then twisted and reached to bring her into his arms. "You'll develop an aversion to kissing."

She yielded, then wriggled clear and reached to push back a heavy coil of short, curly, bronze-coloured hair. It was the same kind of hair her father had. "Better not forget to rub his nose then," she said, swiftly smiled and just as swiftly sprang out of his car. "See you tomorrow, Arthur?"

He had perfect teeth, white and even and very straight. His curly hair was jet-black like his arched brows, but the eyes that amusedly, almost lazily, regarded her from behind the wheel were a very dark and compelling shade of violet. When her mother had called him handsome she hadn't been exaggerating at all.

"I'll be by," he said. "By the way, what have you told your parents?"

"About us?"

"Yes, naturally."

"Well," she said, faltering a little because although she'd told her mother she was going to marry Arthur Cartier, as a matter of fact he'd never actually asked her to marry him. "Well, just that we — think a lot of each other."

He nodded. "And her reaction was . . . ?"

Ellie's dark eyes, inherited from her mother, were a little pensive. "I don't know, Arthur. She smiled, but then she'd do that anyway. She's very gentle and considerate by nature."

He hid a yawn, glanced at his wrist watch and said, "Sure, love. Well, it's late." He straightened behind the wheel. "Till tomorrow."

She stepped back for the car to move away, watched it until it cut down a side road and was lost, then she turned with a little sigh towards the large, perfectly preserved, old house set back across a handsome expanse of garden from the road, and walked thoughtfully onward.

A girl of nineteen in love has every emotion of which she is capable pulled up from deep-down and bared not only to herself but to those who know her best, and before the fires are quenched she is a woman. That is how the transition is made and it is never simple for anyone, but particularly for the girl herself, because in the process of transition from girlhood to womanhood a lot of disturbing judgements have to be made, have to be faced; a lot of illusions are shattered, a whole new world of responsibilities is opened up, and they are invariably somewhat terrifying.

CHAPTER THREE

A TIME OF TRIAL

One thing about a small town that never fails is the capacity people have for accurate gossip. Within three days of the scene at Grandfather Morris's mansion it was known throughout Windsor.

Grandfather Morris, flinty and close-mouthed, could not have been the source. George Jarrett wouldn't have mentioned it. Nor Alice. Nor, because he'd hardly emerged as very heroic, would Carleton have said anything.

There'd been the servants, but since the unpleasantness had occurred beyond their hearing, presumably, at any rate, anyone wishing to seek the actual source would have been driven to consider that Cousin Michael had recounted the tale.

It would have been a fair assumption because Michael was known to, upon occasion, make derisive remarks about the family.

Bu what caused pain wasn't *who* had circulated the tale as much as that it had become common knowledge. Ellie heard it, inevitably, and taxed her mother about it.

"It's so humiliating," she cried to Alice. "Whatever possessed Dad?"

They were in the rear garden, which was Alice's hobby. It was mid-morning and Arthur hadn't arrived although he'd promised the night before, after his date with Ellie, to come by bright and early. Of course that upset Ellie, too, adding a note of harshness to her voice and words.

Alice peeled off her gardening-gloves, rocked back on her heels and raised soft eyes to Ellie. "It goes back a very long time, sweetheart. To your name, in fact."

"My *name*, Mother?"

"It was the name of Grandfather Morris's mother. I've explained that to you. Your father said it was old-fashioned; he wanted to name you Elizabeth so you'd be called Betty. But Grandfather Morris wanted you called Heloise — Ellie."

"I'm beginning to understand, I think."

Alice smiled. "Perhaps. Then it went on, year in, year out. My father is a dominating person, as you know."

"Personality-clash," said Ellie, reaching for a term learned in freshman psychology at college.

Alice nodded and examined the pruning job she'd just completed on a flourishing Queen Elizabeth rose. "I suppose you could sum it up that way, Ellie. But it doesn't seem that simple to me, probably because I've lived with it for so long." Alice smiled, showing small, perfect teeth. "Twenty years *is* a long while, dear."

"But why did he have to say so *much;* it's all over town. I was embarrassed to death when I heard some friends talking about it."

"He is your father, Ellie. He's the kind of man who always feels strongly. I suppose we should really be thankful, otherwise he wouldn't have rebelled at all; he would simply have put his hat on and gone away."

"Mother, Arthur was supposed to come by an hour ago."

Alice gazed at her daughter. "A flat tyre, love. Motor trouble." She shrugged, but deep down she had a sudden sinking feeling. Not because she would care in the slightest if Arthur Cartier *didn't* come for Ellie, but because *if* he didn't come, and if the absence was caused by gossip, Ellie was going to be hurt deeply.

Alice began tugging the gloves back on, looking downward as she did so. Ellie sank down cross-legged on the ground the way she'd sat many times as a child. It gave Alice a nostalgic pang, seeing that undignified but so very natural position.

"What happens now, Mother? I mean, does Daddy still go to the office every day down at Morris & Morris?"

"He doesn't," replied Alice, hefting the pruning shears. "He's opened an office of his own in the Larimore Building on First Street."

Ellie looked blank. "Doing what? All he's ever done is keep books for Morris & Morris."

"Keeping books for the other merchants. As a matter of fact, Ellie, he already has seven accounts." Alice beamed on her daughter. "Last night he told me just before we went to sleep that if he'd had any idea business would have been so promising, he'd have quit ten years ago."

Ellie plucked a blade of grass, glanced at her wrist watch, flung the grass away and put her head slightly to one side in a listening posture.

There was no sound of a car out front.

"Mother, Arthur is thinking of going down to New York," murmured Ellie, keeping her face averted. "That's really where he ought to go, y'know. After all, what has New England to offer a really talented actor, except those little touring troupes, and they're strictly for amateurs."

Alice had no comment to make, nor would she have had a chance to make it because out front a car bounced up into the driveway and came to a halt, and Ellie sprang up and fled in that direction.

She was back in two minutes, leading a tall, easy-moving young man whose name was Morgan Harding, a total stranger, asking to see Mister Jarrett.

Alice gave him directions for reaching the Larimore Building uptown, and said it might save a bit of effort all around if they went indoors where he could telephone first.

He agreed, admired the roses — also admired Ellie, Alice observed — and trooped along towards the back door, saying he'd just got to town from down around Cambridge, was a certified accountant, and had heard there was a new bookkeeping office opening in Windsor, and had driven up on the off-chance of getting a job.

Alice showed him the telephone in the hall, then said, "Well, my husband has only just opened the office, Mister Harding. I doubt very much that the business could stand another man as yet."

Ellie dialled and held out the telephone. "It was a long drive," she said, smiling up into Morgan Harding's face. "You at least deserve being turned down by the boss."

He chuckled and took the telephone, spoke briefly into it, which gave mother and daughter an opportunity to make their inevitable assessments, then he replaced the instrument and with a twinkle in pleasant blue eyes, said, "I'm to come along and have lunch with him. Maybe the strategy is to turn me down on a full stomach. Less traumatic that way."

He seemed so calm, so almost fatalistically poised and capable, Alice felt constrained from being any more pessimistic than she'd already been.

The three of them went out to his car, which was relatively new, dusty and dirty. It wasn't in the same class as a sports car by the wildest stretch of the imagination. He thanked them, climbed in and drove off.

Alice said, "All business. I suppose some day your father will want someone like that. And by then, of course, this particular young man will be long gone. Well, back to my gardening. Come along, you can help for a change."

Ellie let her mother get all the way to the rear-yard gate before she moved to follow. She first made a long slow study of the roadway, which remained absolutely empty despite her strongest yearnings.

There was a slow build-up of filmy clouds across the pale sky. It was springtime in New England, which guaranteed nothing unless it was wildly unpredictable weather, hot then cold, dry then wet, clear then overcast. It seemed now that an overcast was in the making.

Alice was of the opinion that, barring high winds, whatever kind of weather came would be beneficial for her flowers. Ellie moodily worked at her mother's side with little to say. By lunchtime it was quite clear Arthur was not coming.

They went indoors for a snack, and the telephone, Ellie's only remaining link, sat squattily silent. "He would call, certainly," she said, beginning to react to abandonment with hurt pride and anger.

Alice did not intrude. It never helped, trying to soothe someone whose agitation was so obvious. But she hold some personal and private views of Arthur Cartier that weren't very charitable. Still, Ellie *was* her daughter. Her only child in fact. Understandably, then, she couldn't be charitable.

Just before mother and daughter finished their luncheon dishes the telephone finally rang and Ellie raced for it.

It was her father calling to cheerfully report

that he'd hired Morgan Harding, whose qualifications, he enthused, were excellent. Ellie wordlessly handed the telephone to her mother and fled to her room.

Alice, showing anxiety in her eyes if not in her voice, watched their daughter while she listened to George. Finally, she said, "I'm sure you know best. If you *need* Mister Harding, love. . . ."

George chuckled. Alice had always been tactful. "I can use him now, and within another month I'll have more than enough to keep us both busy. Another thing; he's experienced at tax-form preparation. Don't forget that income tax time is only a little while off." He paused, then said, "I landed two more nice accounts this morning."

That reassured her. "I'm awfully glad, George."

His enthusiasm was suddenly checked as he said, "You don't sound like yourself. Is something wrong?"

"Well. Ellie learned through friends this morning about the scene at Grandfather's house last week. It upset her. Then there is something else: Arthur Cartier was supposed to drop by, and didn't show up."

George said, "Him."

Alice's intuitive sixth-sense pricked up. "George, there something I should know?"

"Maybe. We'll discuss it when I get home this evening. Got to go now."

As Alice rang off she had a premonition. Standing as she was, in the little hallway with her daughter's closed bedroom door in plain sight, she had a feeling that her husband knew something about Arthur Cartier he had been holding back.

Oddly enough, since he was a man who invariably kept his word, although he'd sworn to make inquiries about Arthur the night of the unpleasantness a week before, he'd not ever again mentioned Arthur's name.

She knew her husband. If George had discovered something it had to be pretty bad for him not to mention it at all.

A wife somewhere, maybe?

She turned with reluctance to go back into the rear-yard. Her strongest instinct was to go instead to her daughter with soothing comfort. But she didn't.

Outside, that filmy overcast was beginning to firm up, to turn into a kind of vaguely sooty gathering of definite clouds. The stillness was utter, the air was heavy, a promise of something, rain perhaps, was in the offing.

Whatever came couldn't be prevented, so Alice went back to her gardening, only now instead of her chosen pastime, it was a discipline.

She almost forgot about the additional bookkeeping accounts George had got. They were, however, the only cheerful events of this day, so she finally recalled his pleasure over them and smiled a little as she worked.

By the time of day she was due to start supper

those clouds had come all together, had congealed into a low, gloomy overcast with threatening dark edges all round.

She went indoors, lit some lights, went to shower and change, and when she returned to the kitchen Ellie was also freshly scrubbed and dressed, ready to help. Her cheerfulness, such a contrast to her earlier mood, only made Alice the more conscious of the secret pain.

It was frustrating for Alice. She *knew* the right words and naturally her sympathies were warm and outgoing, but common sense held her back. She worked beside Ellie wearing a smile, unwilling to open any flood-gates by mentioning Ellie's anguish.

By the time George got home Alice was prepared to believe anything he had to tell her about Arthur Cartier; even that he'd deserted a wife and perhaps several babies somewhere.

But it was more prosaic. It was long after the evening meal was over and past and they were upstairs preparing for bed that he said, "About the time Arthur inherited that money Ellie told us about, he also started dating John Forrest's daughter. Alice, that coincided with the time Ellie said they were going to get married. In other words, this man was seeing the daughter of the attorney, Forrest, and at the same time he was making promises to Ellie."

Alice, already conditioned to her logical reaction, sat at the dressing table regarding the hairbrush in her hand, and said, "My father was right, George."

He shot her a look, then said gently, "Not entirely, sweetheart. Your father said *all* actors were bums — or words to that effect. All this proves is that *one* actor is a bum. And I'll tell you something else, too — the next time I catch him around this house, I'll. . . . Well, I don't know — but I'll do *something!*"

CHAPTER FOUR

MEETINGS AND ADJUSTMENTS

The rain arrived the night of the day George Jarrett hired Morgan Harding. It was not recorded in local weather journals quite that way, however.

It also began raining the night of the day Arthur Cartier neglected, through whatever reason, to keep his appointment with Ellie Jarrett.

By morning enough water had fallen to drench the town and its surrounding countryside, but as a matter of fact people welcomed a decent spring rain. For one thing, spring downpours were usually warm. This was exactly the type of rainfall farmers most earnestly prayed for; warm rainwater soaking chilly earth caused the temperate reaction that triggered new growth.

Alice could see from her kitchen window how the roses responded. A fresh vigour was noticeable; a kind of reawakening that no amount of domestic watering ever quite approximated.

Of course there were drawbacks. For one thing the car George Jarrett had inadvertently left standing in the driveway the night before, instead of putting in the garage, suffered condensation of the distributor which no amount of drying with rags seemed to alleviate, and as George's temper slowly rose, Alice turned the preparation of breakfast over to Ellie, went to the hall telephone and, on the off-chance a zealous new employee might already be at the office, called down there.

He was. He also agreed to drive out at once and pick George up.

Afterwards, with admirable timing, Alice was busy in the kitchen almost to the minute before Morgan Harding drove up outside, then she ran forth to tell her husband he was coming.

George probably had not liked what she'd done, but with Morgan standing there he couldn't very well say so. She insured he couldn't say anything at the breakfast table either by inviting Morgan to come and eat with them. He had already breakfasted, he said, so she insisted he have a cup of coffee. He agreed, and, oddly enough, when all four of them were at the table, instead of a sour mood prevailing, even Ellie perked up. Morgan told her she was even more beautiful in early morning than she was in late afternoon.

George looked at his new employee suspiciously, but said nothing. Alice understood the look if neither of the younger people had. George, never capable of gallantry himself, had frequently said men who knew exactly what to say to women were gigolos at heart.

But it was difficult to look at Morgan Harding, who was wide-shouldered, poised and capable-seeming, and envision a gigolo.

When the meal was over and the men departed,

Ellie, while helping her mother with the dishes, said thoughtfully that she thought Mister Harding was handsome. Alice concurred, but she also thought she understood what was behind that remark: the vindictiveness of a hurt child. She was right, too.

The rain turned to drizzle about noon or shortly before, which helped visibility, cleansed the air, and washed house- and store-fronts. It was during this period that Arthur Cartier drove up, his little red sports car glistening. Alice saw the car first and went to tell Ellie, who'd been straightening her room.

Ellie greeted Arthur at the front door with a quizzical little smile and he kissed her cheek as he stepped inside. "Just couldn't make it yesterday," he told her. "You know how those thing are, sometimes."

Ellie may have known but she didn't look as though she did. They went into the parlour where Arthur paused before a wall mirror, then, evidently satisfied with its reflection, crossed over to take a seat on the sofa beside Ellie.

"You could have telephoned, Arthur," she said quietly, unable despite her obvious relief to quite conceal her annoyance.

He flashed those perfect teeth and lifted a hand to trace out the cupid-bow shape of her mouth. "Don't be shrewish, love. I ran into an old friend uptown. He was on his way through, bound for Montreal, where he'd heard there was an outstanding amateur troupe. You'll understand how those things are, when you've been around show business for as long as I have, Ellie. One sees an opportunity, and one must ruthlessly seize it."

"What opportunity, Arthur?"

"That's what took up most of the day, love. We talked. He's putting together this new show. An off-Broadway production. That's why he was heading for Montreal. He wants fresh faces, new songs, an entirely fresh innovation. He wants me to try out for second-heavy. That is, for the role of supporting lead-actor. We went over the script, had luncheon at the hotel, then spent the afternoon wrangling." Arthur's magnificent smile returned. "He doesn't have all the financing yet, you see, so I dangled the bait; I'd participate somewhat, in exchange for the right to make some small changes." Arthur threw up his hands. "Do you understand?"

She thought so, and perhaps it had been selfish to expect him to take a moment out to telephone her. On the other hand, she knew for a fact that her father had taken time out from important conferences to call her mother. Still, as Arthur kept telling her, actors were a different kind of people; they weren't to be held accountable. The staid virtues did not apply to them. They were creative, they were artists, they were a step or two above the common herd of people. Responsibility, accountability, morality, the restraining forces that kept little people perennially little, could scarcely be applied to actors and actresses.

She soberly considered his beautiful features,

masculine in every respect, yet so perfect they might have been created by a sculptor, and she melted towards him as she always had.

"Did anything definite come of it all?" she asked a faint sinking sensation holding her gravely still on the sofa while she awaited the answer she dreaded to hear.

"Quite probably," he replied. "He'll go on up to Montreal today and be back in a week. Then I'll have his answer."

"And if the answer is favourable, Arthur?"

He caught one of her hands and held it. "Look, love, what's so terrible about my going down to New York? We've already discussed that, haven't we? I mean, what is there for someone with my talent in New England? Isn't success what we want for me?"

She nodded, but she wasn't thinking in terms of success, she was thinking in terms of loss.

"Well then, suppose we hop into my car and drive uptown for luncheon some place?"

"All right. I'll get my raincoat."

He rose still holding her hand, drew her up with him and used his other hand to tilt her chin. "Don't be so prosaic, Ellie. New Englanders and their raincoats are so plebeian. Anyway, it's only a drizzle and it'll look like pearls in your hair, like wine on your lips, like diamond-chips on your lashes." He gave her a little tug. "Come along."

She went, and willingly, for he had the ability to recall lines from plays that thrilled her to the heart. He was so worldly, so heady to be with, so blithe and beautiful.

She failed to see her mother at the dining-room window as they ran to the car, dived in to avoid getting too wet, and laughed in unison as he revved the motor and swung the car through the leaden day with its glistening roads and sidewalks, its sombre and dripping wet trees and its murky-grey but not unpleasant light.

There was no other sensation she could imagine that equalled being with him. Emotion was heaped upon emotion. She was jealous when other girls turned for a second, long look as he passed them with Ellie at his side. She was regally proud the way waiters bowed, the way stuffy people wearing proper waistcoats and ties oggled him with fishy stares of suspicion and disapproval, the way her friends showed definite envy. And of course when his practised hands and lips sought her, the thrill was heart-deep, soul-searing.

She rarely returned from an outing with him that she didn't feel drained dry with exhaustion. He played on her emotions with the exquisite lightness of a perfectionist. If she ever really thought about the experience he had to have to possess all this knowledgeability and poise, she attributed it to his acting career.

He was, as he kept telling her, different.

They ate at a little any place called The Purple Happening, Windsor's only genuine coffee house, and there she encountered dark and sultry Jane Forrest, with whom she'd attended secondary school but who had afterwards been lost in New York for two years.

It was the way Jane ran her fingers through Arthur's hair, and the way she'd smiled directly into his eyes, that shocked Ellie.

Afterwards he passed it off with a pleased little shrug and although she was aware of his prominent ego, this time his pleasure was too obvious.

"Old friends," he told her, as their meal arrived. "Jane's got something going for her, love."

"So I see," said Ellie drily. "Be sure it isn't you, Arthur."

He raised brilliant eyes. "A bit jealous are you, duck?" He chuckled. "Good thing, now and then. Keeps a woman on her toes."

"An Italian woman would have knifed Jane just now for the way she looked at you."

"But you are a proper New Englander, aren't you?"

It sounded faintly ironic, as though he were throwing something in her face. She responded as much to that as to Jane Forrest.

"Don't bet on it, Arthur."

Now he laughed aloud, bringing all eyes to their table. She blushed, dropped her head and started pushing food into her mouth that was utterly tasteless. For a moment she hated him, but that passed and, as always, she felt herself being buffeted and punished by those surging, unchecked emotions.

He invariably did that to her. Even when they were alone he had the ability to dredge up every ounce of turmoil of which she was capable. Perhaps an older woman would have considered it just too exhausting, but at nineteen, Ellie Jarrett, with the full resiliency of youth, knew only that it was living right up to the brink with each and every breath.

"Forget it," he said, his tone soothing and conciliatory. "Jane's a hungry girl. Incidentally, she also tried hard to prove herself an actress down in New York."

A suspicion formed and Ellie said, raising her face, "By any chance, love, did Janie happen to figure in your talk with that producer yesterday?"

He gazed at her briefly, then blushed faintly as he said, "Janie Forrest isn't in that league, love. She never will be. She's got home-town talent but not Broadway talent."

It wasn't a definite answer but it was just derogatory enough to pacify Ellie. She didn't even realise he hadn't actually answered her until, hours later back home with the rain coming down in torrents again, she went back over their time together bit by bit.

But by then she was tired and over-reacting; was willing to accept his slight derogation of Jane Forrest's talent as an oblique answer. Also by then her mother's conversation kept interrupting the train of thought that otherwise would have kept her moodily quiet until suppertime.

She gave it up, finally, satisfied he *hadn't* answered, but also a little weary of the entire interlude as well.

Alice said, "Wonder of wonders, Ellie: Morgan Harding went forth this afternoon without knowing a soul in town, and got another two accounts for the Jarrett company. Isn't that amazing?"

Ellie was polite enough to agree. As a matter of fact it really *was* amazing; Windsor, like all insular New England towns, had its prejudice against outsiders. Even other New England outsiders. For a total stranger to arrive in town one day and successfully solicit business the next day was slightly more than amazing; it was also unheard of.

"Your father was terribly pleased," said Alice, and it very gradually dawned upon Ellie that her mother, in discussing the things of interest that had happened this day, was very resolutely avoiding any mention of Arthur Cartier.

That was the first inkling Ellie had that her mother did not like Arthur. It surprised her. Alice had always in the past been tolerant, friendly and hospitable to her friends, of both sexes.

But of course Arthur was different. That would account for it. Even in some uninhibited place such as Hollywood, he'd be recognised as different, but in a place like Windsor . . . Ellie had to smile to herself.

CHAPTER FIVE

DIFFERENT KINDS OF MEN

A most unusual meeting occurred four days later, when the sun was out again and the world was bursting with fresh-watered new life. Morgan Harding ambled into the coffee house — The Purple Happening — while Ellie was at lunch there with Arthur.

That was somewhat unusual, at least Ellie considered it so since Morgan, according to her father, was a very dependable, stable, solid-citizen type. She'd have thought he'd have had his lunch at one of the local restaurants where the business men ate.

Perhaps, ordinarily, he would have have, but today, slumming or not, he appeared at The Purple Happening with a genial smile, saw her and ambled over to say, "I was wondering what drew me to this place."

She smiled, introduced him to Arthur, then made a nervous little uncertain suggestion that he might join them. She and Arthur had been arguing mildly; she wasn't at all sure Arthur would approve but she'd been raised to be polite.

Morgan saved her the embarrassment. "Thanks, but I'll take one of the corner tables where I can look around. I had no idea there'd be such a place in Windsor."

That seemed to irritate Arthur, who looked up without smiling. "It's a backward town all right, but I believe in the modern generation you can expect to find acceptable restaurants anywhere, Mister Harding."

Morgan's smiling, confident eyes dropped to Arthur's face and lingered. "I'm sure I can," he said, in an almost lazily bantering tone. "Usually they're discernible by odour as well as by sight, eh?"

That brought colour to Arthur's cheeks and a quick, yeasty flash to his beautiful eyes. Morgan lightly touched Ellie's shoulder, nodded and strolled away leaving Arthur hanging there with something to say and no one to say it to.

He watched Morgan all the way across the room. "Who *is* that insufferable square?"

"An accountant who works with my father. Morgan Harding. He's from Cambridge."

"Of course," said Arthur, turning back to his meal, each word dripping with scorn. "He *would* be from Cambridge — or some similar place."

Ellie didn't like that scorn, but she actually knew Morgan Harding so casually that in spite of a natural urge to defend him against Arthur, she simply said, "What's wrong with Cambridge?"

Arthur didn't deign to answer. He merely made a gesture with one hand, indicating contempt. Then he said, "By the way, love, they tell me your father's bouncing back phenomenally well after being booted out by your grandfather. I'm a great admirer of the free-enterprise spirit, myself."

That annoyed her, too, so she said, "Then you must like Mister Harding. He's a free-enterpriser, too, love."

The beautiful dark violet eyes came up slowly and got a little narrow. "Are you needling me, Ellie?"

She had been, of course, but she instantly quailed before his quiet anger. "Forget Mister Harding, Arthur, and my father's business. Tell me about us."

His expression changed slightly but not very much, and the narrowed eyes kept staring directly at her. "What about us, Ellie?"

"Well, has the producer returned from Montreal yet; has it been decided when you'll be leaving for New York — and do I go with you or follow after?"

He dropped his glance and picked a moment at his food before saying, "I see. As a matter of fact the producer won't be back in Windsor until day after tomorrow. I had a telegram from him last night. Of course that answers the other questions, too, doesn't it? I mean, how can we arrive at any definite conclusions until we know whether I'm even going to New York?"

She smiled, relieved because the unpleasant interlude was past, and also because there would be no definite answer to the other question just yet either, although why she should have felt relief about this was puzzling. He'd said he loved her a dozen times. He'd never once ruled out the feasibility of taking her to New York with him.

But nevertheless she had a deep and abiding fear on that score.

She was aware of Morgan Harding over across the room, was aware that occasionally he turned and studied her. When he finally departed she lifted her face, followed his progress, then saw Arthur gazing at her with an expression of sceptical interest.

"A *book-keeper?*" he said, making it sound equivalent to a child-molester. Then he gave her his handsome, lazy smile again, reproving her with it for looking at another man when he was so close by.

"My father happens to be a book-keeper," she replied.

His mood was conciliatory. "Well, of course, we need this kind of person." He left no doubt, however, that *he* considered them somewhat less than indispensable. "Drab, colourless, duck; men for no season putting in their time between birth and death seeking and worshipping security."

"And raising families," she said. "And paying taxes. And fighting wars to protect Liberty. And obeying the laws. *And* supporting the performing arts, Arthur."

He threw up his hands in a gesture of defeat. "You win, love. Mister What's-his-name is the salt of the earth." He laughed. "I intended no disrespect towards your father in any case. I just didn't see that other chap — Harding as someone worth your interest."

She could have defended Morgan Harding on that score, too. She, who rarely actually spoke out against his sneering contempt for people other than actors and actresses, was definitely in a rebellious mood now.

The reason she controlled herself was basic; she was afraid to lose him. They had never had a real quarrel, although at first they'd had disputes, and she did not want to quarrel with him now. Not this close to whatever was coming next in their relationship.

She had a feeling, too, that if they quarrelled now it would be the end of everything. He hadn't said anything to make her feel this way. In fact he seemed no different than he'd ever been. Nevertheless, she had that deep-down feeling. It more than frightened her, it saddened her, too.

"Forget it," he said, smiling at her. "Look, I've got to run a few errands this afternoon, so maybe I'd better run you home, love. All right?"

"Yes." She rose from the table thinking he'd mentioned no errands earlier.

They got outside before she began feeling tired. Not physically tired as though she'd been waterskiing or mountain-climbing, but drained in some more subtle way.

On the drive home she didn't say much and when he kissed her at the kerbing then sped away, back towards the heart of town, she was relieved to be alone.

The house was empty. Her mother had put a roast in the oven. Its aroma permeated each room. There were fresh-cut flowers in the sun-room, which lay just off the large old parlour, while beyond the windows birds sang in the large old trees which gave summer-shade to the property.

Ellie kicked off her shoes and went slowly through the house, feeling the smooth-grained walls, the banisters, the jambs and sills and floors underfoot. She'd first seen the light of day in this house. All her life up to now had been spent here, except for the periods when she was away at college.

She loved the rooms, the shadows, the safety and the security. She even loved the serene and friendly silences.

She dropped into a large chair with legs curled beneath her. What was so terrible about security?

A heavy hand dropped across the front door with unexpected suddenness. She gave a start, then sank back waiting for her heartbeat to return to normal.

The heavy hand rolled down across the wood one more time.

She rose barefoot and went to see who was on the porch. It was Morgan Harding with a broad smile. "Your father asked me to come by for some papers he left on the desk in his study."

Ellie stepped aside for him to enter. Until then she hadn't realised just how tall he really was. Of course it helped this illusion, that she was barefoot, but at the moment she didn't think of that. He kept looking at her, so she stepped past to lead the way.

Her father's study was a converted storeroom which, until he'd added panelling and rear-wall windows, had reminded Ellie of pictures of dungeons she'd seen as a child.

In fact, even after he'd lighted it with the windows she still retained that earlier feeling of uneasiness in the room. Of course, being much older now, she wasn't conscious of that discomfort while being in the room. Or perhaps it was the wide shoulders and easy confidence of her companion that kept her from even thinking of the childhood fear.

He went to the desk, glanced once at a large envelope, then scooped it up. "Right where he said it was, Miss Jarrett." The friendly eyes remained on her face. That man you were having lunch with — is he your fiancé?"

She supposed it was a fair question, but all the same she didn't appreciate its implication of intimacy. "We have been good friends for quite a while, Mister Harding."

He nodded, reproved. "All right. I'm put in my place. I'm an employee of your father. I understand."

That was ridiculous. Whatever other faults she might have, being the least bit snobbish was not included. Class-consciousness was something that just had never arisen in her environment, or if it had around town, she'd managed to be quite ignorant of its existence.

"Don't be silly," she said, smiling because his attitude was just too preposterous. "Whoever you work for couldn't possibly mean anything to me. Unless it was a Mafia chieftain or something like that." She led the way back to the parlour, swung and faced him. "It just didn't seem to me we really knew each other that well, Mister Harding."

He grinned. "I'm curious. I'm nosy, if your prefer that term."

She cocked her head. "Which term fits?"

"Neither, actually. Curiosity implies nosiness. My *real* feeling is interest. It's worlds different from plain curiosity."

"Semantics," she answered, beginning to feel a little uncomfortable with him.

"No such thing," he exclaimed. "I'm interested because you are beautiful. Because you are single. Because you are — just you." He kept smiling down at her. "Curiosity wouldn't cover the same ground."

"Would being interested in me also cover the fact that I might have a fiancé, Mister Harding?"

He laughed, and for the first time she noticed the latent fire in the depths of his eyes. It was a masculine, yeasty, smouldering. "It would," he said. "And it would also make me resent him."

She glanced round towards the front door. The ground they were verbally treading was becoming suspiciously like quicksand. He recaptured her attention by saying that since she had noticeably skirted around actually saying she was engaged, he thought it would be genuinely hospitable if she'd take pity on a poor stranger and show him around Windsor.

"Just once," he averred. "Just this one evening. After all, if *you* were a stranger in Cambridge and *I* saw you wandering in bewilderment, I'd do as much for you."

She almost smiled. "For someone allegedly wandering in bewilderment, Mister Harding, you've managed to find The Purple Happening. Beyond that place, Windsor just doesn't have too much to offer."

"My sense of direction is terrible. I could get lost."

They both smiled over that. Windsor just wasn't a place anyone could get lost in. The town wasn't that huge, and beyond the town all a person had to do was climb one of the little tree-topped knobs in order to see in every direction.

He tried again. "I'm lonely."

That, of course, was more plausible, except that he just wasn't the kind of a man who would brood. "You," she told him, "wouldn't be lonely in Timbuktu."

"Well. You see, I have this childhood fear of going to motion picture theatres alone. Rather like claustrophobia, I think. Yet there is a picture playing uptown that I've always wanted to see-and. . . . Would you?"

"Mister Harding, what is the name of that picture?"

He floundered badly. So badly in fact they both laughed, and as he held the envelope in both hands she finally said, "All right. Is seven o'clock agreeable?"

"Perfect."

"I'll be ready and waiting."

He perked up, strode to the door, turned back and said, "You've made my day."

After he'd gone Ellie went on into her own room with a little lilting feeling of comfortable warmth. He might not have been very smooth, but he was certainly amusing, likeable, easy to be around. He didn't dominate and yet he managed some way to win in the end.

She rummaged a closet for what she'd wear to the theatre with him. It was while she was doing that the correct definition came to mind.

Persistence. Morgan Harding was persistent.

CHAPTER SIX

UNDER A TROUBLED MOON

Her mother seemed unusually enthusiastic over her date with Morgan Harding, and of course her father, who had taken her side in her friendship with Arthur Cartier, was perfectly in accord with this change.

By the time Morgan arrived dinner was over, George and Alice Jarrett were discreetly absent — watching television in the sunroom, actually — and Ellie was dressed in something cashmere-soft and clinging that made his eyes brighten with quick, sparkling appreciation.

"I have excellent taste," he told her with mock gravity. "I don't believe there's another woman in this town as handsome as you are, Miss Jarrett."

She responded with a mockery of her own. She curtsied and dropped her eyes and said in a simper, "Oh, Mister Harding, I bet you tell that to all the girls."

They left the house, strode towards his car — freshly washed and polished, she noticed — climbed in and drove off. Around them lay the vestiges of a perfect springtime night. She kept waiting for her conscience to rear up, but it never did. At least not for as long as they were alone together; when it perhaps *should* have troubled her, it did not.

The theatre was dark, full, and noisy. They didn't reach their seats until the feature film was well under way. Not that it mattered much, since the plot had to do with two men struggling against one another for the love of the same girl.

She leaned close to whisper. "Now I understand perfectly why you simply *had* to see this picture. It has such an absorbingly different plot."

He picked up her hand and held it. Otherwise there was nothing especially objectionable nor commendable about the evening, thus far.

Her attention wandered from time to time. Of course there were people she'd know in the seats, but at the moment it was too dark to see them, and along towards the end of the picture, when her companion seemed to squirm, she was just as ready to escape as he was.

They drove the lighted streets of central Windsor. She pointed out several of the oldest business establishments, forgetting that he'd been canvassing for her father's new business, and probably was almost as familiar with the interiors as she was.

She also showed him the new secondary school, Windsor's pride and joy. She guided him to Old Town, which was a westerly suburb with brass plates nailed to the fronts of fairly well-preserved old homes, indicating in one instance where Windsor's first surgery had stood, where a Confederate spy had been run to earth during the War Between The States, and finally, with an expression of mixed feeling, she pointed out her grandfather's old mansion on top of its elegant little landscaped knob.

Morgan nodded at that old house, lighted now and looking very aloof, very forbidding. "Y'know," he told her. "I've set a goal for myself. Someday I'm going to walk up there, sell Mister Morris on letting skilled specialists handle the Morris & Morris bookkeeping, and walk out of there with all his auditing and accounting business."

She smiled, a little tartly. "It's a very noble ambition. Have you ever met my grandfather?"

"No. But I've heard an awful lot of him."

"From my father?"

"Not a word. I get my information from secret sources."

She wrinkled her nose at him. "I can imagine. I think Windsor has more gossips per square mile than any other town in New England."

He thought on that as he engaged gears and cruised northward from out front of Grandfather Morris's residence. "Maybe. It's not important."

"It can hurt," she replied, offering a kind of quiet rebuttal. "Tales about my grandfather and father getting into an argument hurt us all."

"You're making mountains out of molehills. That was a long time ago."

"A month?"

"Sure," he said, swinging up the north-country

pike out of town. "A month is a lifetime in the world of gossip. For instance, today who remembers, except perhaps your family? No one. Do you know what the big rumour is now? The governor is going to be divorced by his wife. A very shocking thing even in our permissive age, by New England standards."

She had heard that tale. Had, in fact, been assured that it was not just a rumour but was an imminent fact. And it *was* interesting; she thought there hadn't ever before been a governor divorced anywhere in New England while he was in office.

Morgan slowed, looked down, then grinned triumphantly. "You see? Even you're caught up with this new thing. And next month — what? Something else just as diverting." He drove to the wide verge where weak moonlight limned the ancient hills as they retreated, rank after low rank of them, up in the general direction of Canada, stopped the car and leaned in sprawling comfort behind the wheel. "I'll tell you what I think: With you everything is serious."

She looked up quickly. "Most things *are* serious." She was piqued.

"Not so, lovely lady. Most things are amusing, troublesome, wearisome, angering, surprising, but never very serious."

"Are you a flower-child, Mister Harding?"

That, and the scowl accompanying it, made him roar with laughter. "Would I be practising my trade if I were? Look, Ellie, I'm a realist, but not one of those monumentally self-centred ones. I don't see my private heartbreak bringing down a black blight upon the countryside. I'm not here on earth to command legions nor right all the wrongs. I'm just not that important and neither are you. So we learn to laugh a little, to roll with the punches a little, to live and let live — and to seek our own end of each rainbow."

"You're not an accountant, Mister Harding, you're a frustrated philosopher."

He grinned. "If you wish. And what are you, Ellie?"

He was looking straight down into her upturned face, his ruggedly handsome features gentle, amused, poised and confident. She'd never met a man like him before. She couldn't even very honestly compare him to Arthur. There just was no basis for such a comparison. But of course, since Arthur was the bright centre of her emotional universe, she would eventually have to make that comparison.

"Well," he said softly, "what are you, Ellie? A fragile glass-house orchid, a tough New England Yankee? Are you one of those inhibited people who hang out in places like The Purple Happening trying to convince everyone, but mostly yourself, that you're terribly mod, terribly *un*inhibited?"

She didn't know how to answer him. The frustration was so real she felt tears burning behind her eyelids. "Let's go back," she said coldly. "What I am — I suppose I simply am, and that's all there can be to it."

He made no move to start the car. "You are right," he exclaimed. "And hanging out in a dump like The Purple Happening can't change you one bit, Ellie. You're not arty. You don't want to blow your mind. You don't see yourself as the foci of all things. Put another way — you're not a mental pygmy nor an exhibitionist with a distorted vision of your value. You don't belong."

She had a feeling about him. "Why the lecture, Mister Harding? Did you decide, after watching me at luncheon, my soul needs saving. Are you some kind of missionary group of one dedicated to saving me from myself?"

"Naw. I'm just a guy with both feet on the same ground as everyone else, who isn't too much of a coward to see what makes the big greeny ball go round and round."

"A square?"

He nodded. "If you like. It's a *passé* description, but if you like I'm a square. So are you. Do you know where we differ? I'm honest and you're not."

Now he reached, spun the motor to life, and after craning to make certain no cars were approaching, he made a great, illegal turning and ended up heading back in the direction of Windsor.

She said nothing.

For a long while he was just as silent, but when the outskirts of town crept out with all lights burning, he shot her a look, wagged his head and said, "Sure ended up a wild night, didn't it? I wanted to make a good impression. Instead. . . ." He shrugged, looked at her again, and went silent.

They were almost in front of her parents' house before she spoke to him again. It was to ask a question. "I've never gone out with an evangelist before, Mister Harding, and I'd like some clarification. Was all that oratory just for me, or is it a line you use right along in your wrestles with Satan?"

"Just you. I'm no proselyter, Ellie." He reached across, opened the door and waited for her to get out at the opposite side of the car. She did, and he climbed out on his own side, strolled round and said, "If I was the least bit interested in wrestling Satan, Ellie, when that character you were having luncheon with got annoyed with me, I'd have wrestled then and there. If ever there was an imp, he's it."

"Arthur Cartier is *not* an imp!"

"Big, fat phony," said Harding, and moved with the speed of a striking snake to catch her arm at the wrist just inches before her blow would have exploded against his cheek.

He smiled crookedly, a trifle cruelly, as he forced her arm down then released it. "Baby, baby, you're so blind it's tragic." He stepped back. "Thanks for showing me the town. Goodnight."

He went back to the car, climbed in and drove off with just one last, slow smile thrown back towards her.

She stood in late-night chill for a bit, then turned and went slowly on up to the darkened house.

The part that rankled most, of course, was the truth. She resolutely told herself there wasn't very *much* truth in anything he'd said, but there had been *some*. There usually was some truth on both sides when people disagreed.

But the most preposterous thing of all was his appraisal of Arthur. It was simply inconceivable that Morgan Harding could make a judgement when he'd only met Arthur once.

To do a thing like that a man had to be a supreme egotist. What could *possibly* give Morgan any idea he was qualified to judge Arthur at all; even if they'd known one another, how could someone as utterly mundane as an accountant even begin to understand someone as gifted, talented, as monumentally different as Arthur!

She got into the house silently, removed her shoes and went soundlessly to her own room with its rear window and its familiar objects. She didn't light even the bedside lamp, but undressed in starlight, scrubbed her face, creamed it, caught her hair severely back, knotted it into place and stood in the soft-sad non-luminous waning starlight with a distant memory disturbing her. Grandfather Morris, who was tough and shrewd and wise about such things, had once made a remark in her presence that she'd never forgot and which came now to make a crack in the solid wall of defence she'd erected around Arthur.

Grandfather Morris had said, "There never was a man made that other men couldn't read, evaluate, respect or distrust, all within fifteen minutes. And there was never a woman who could really and accurately dissect a man until after she'd married him. And some are so blind and stupid they don't even see what empty shells they have even after two decades of married life."

The point was, of course, that Morgan Harding, according to Grandfather Morris's philosophy, was better qualified to judge Arthur Cartier than *she* was, and Harding didn't even know Arthur.

Despite a lifelong characteristic of respect for Grandfather Morris's traditional — in the family at any rate — infallibility, Ellie thought as she turned towards her bed, she had caught him in an error.

She would have closed her eyes upon that conviction and gone to sleep except that something else came now to bother her: '. . . Do you know where we differ? I'm honest and you're not!'

She *did* have doubts about Arthur. She'd *always* had them. She had mistrust as well.

She threw back the covers, sat up and looked out where that non-luminous softness lay.

She *would* be honest with herself. She *had* to be, because shortly now there was to be a crisis. Whether it was over his departure for New York and the supporting-lead role in the off-Broadway production, or something less glamorous, she didn't know. But she could feel very plainly that *something* — *some* kind of crucial epoch — was hurtling towards her, and it most certainly involved Arthur, her love for him, his love for her — and possibly it even involved Morgan Harding, too. But just at this moment she couldn't believe *that* was so.

CHAPTER SEVEN

THE SPONTANEOUS CONSPIRACY

Ellie tried three times to contact Arthur before remembering it was the day the producer was back in town. Afterwards, she gave it up. Arthur might be anywhere with his companion, the local hotel, driving in the soothing up-country, or perhaps down by the distant river. She only knew, because she'd heard Arthur say it several times, that only very prosaic, mundane people met in stuffy little offices or in colourless little restaurants, to discuss business.

She forced herself to be patient even though she most certainly did not feel that way. She was quite sure that today, or at the very latest tomorrow, would change her life. Under those circumstances it was easy to understand her anxiety.

Alice was discreetly curious about the outcome of Ellie's date with Morgan Harding. Ellie wouldn't say much, except that Morgan was very opinionated.

About noon Grandfather Morris called to say he would like to come round this evening. Alice was so surprised she forgot to relay this message to her husband until Ellie, smiling, said, "Mother, it's not really an apocalypse. Grandfather used to come over quite often. And you'd better telephone Dad, hadn't you?"

Later in the afternoon Ellie went shopping uptown with her mother. They had finished grocery-shopping and were standing out front of a chic little dress shop window when a man's smooth, amiable voice addressed them from back a short distance near the kerbing.

Morgan Harding stood there, smiling. "I'm on my way for afternoon coffee. It'd make my entire day if you two would join me."

Alice was flattered and pleased, no doubt of it, but she did something that caught Ellie unprepared. She said, "Mister Harding, you are most kind, but you see I've got one more little urgent errand, so I'll beg off this time. You and Ellie run along. Ellie, I'll see you back at the car."

Morgan probably did not understand Alice's strategy even though he made no very concerted effort to thwart it. Instead, he reached over, took Ellie's arm through his arm and started tugging her along. "I've been wondering lately," he said, "if you couldn't show me some of the better places to swim over along the river. It keeps getting a little warmer each day. Summer'll be all over the place soon now, won't it?"

"Don't ever count on New England weather in springtime," she answered, side-stepping the main issue as they entered a small restaurant and got a little out-of-the-way table. "One day it'll be simply beautiful, the very next day there'll be wind and sleet."

"I'm perfectly willing to run the risk."

Their coffee came and Ellie looked critically at Morgan as he reached for his cup. "I'm not," she said.

His hand stopped moving. It was the reaction she'd looked for. She smiled very sweetly at him.

"I'm not an honest person, remember, Mister Harding? You wouldn't want to be seen with someone like me."

She sipped coffee, gazed at the other patrons of the café, recognised several, nodded at a few who were staring, then put the cup down and pointedly glanced at her watch.

He said, "I'll come by for you on Sunday."

Their eyes met and held. She was mildly surprised at his boldness and also slightly annoyed. "Don't bother. I'll be busy Sunday."

"I have to come by anyway," he informed her. "Your father and I are working on an over-all bookkeeping and auditing system for Morris & Morris."

Remembering her grandfather's telephone call, also recalling something Morgan had said the last time they were together, she began to feel interested. "Did you actually get the Morris & Morris account?"

He grinned. "Not exactly. I bulldozed my way in to see your grandfather. I told you I'd do that someday. It was pretty hectic for a bit, he's a cantankerous old gentleman when he wants to be."

"Or when he's intruded upon, Mister Harding."

He nodded. "That's right. And it *was* an intrusion. But I knew I had something to sell him that would modernise Morris & Morris, something he should at least *look* at."

She impishly smiled in spite of herself at a vision of this tall, wide-shouldered, very earnest man regaling her cursing, fist-shaking, domineering old grandfather. "It must have been something to see," she said.

His eyes twinkled a bit ruefully. "Well, if he'd been fifty years younger I think he'd have heaved me out bodily."

"And he agreed to try your system?"

"Not exactly. He agreed to *consider* it. I didn't ask any more than that."

She speculated. Doubtless Grandfather Morris's reason for wishing to see her father tonight had something to do with this. She debated whether or not to tell Morgan of this impending visit, and finally, knowing her father and grandfather were like flint on steel, she thought of Morgan's capacity for control, for tact, for understanding, and said, "I think I could help, if you just weren't such an opinionated person."

He studied her face a moment before saying, "Look, Ellie, everything I said to you the other night was true. You can delude yourself into believing otherwise if you wish. I'm not going to repeat any of it again. I simply saw someone heading for a smash-up, put in my two-bits worth in the hope of at least slowing down the process, and that, love, was that."

"You were so — insufferably righteous, so opinionated."

"I apologise. I didn't want you hurt. But I apologise, and I promise, unless you ask me, never to butt into your affairs again."

She nodded. "Fair enough. Now listen, my grandfather is coming over to see my father tonight. It'll be their first face-to-face meeting since their big fight a month or so ago. I would guess Grandfather wants to discuss this business arrangement you've been telling me about."

"Possibly. Where do I fit in?"

"You just happen by tonight after seven. My father and grandfather are very likely to start arguing again. You could sort of guide things, couldn't you? I mean, if their hang-up is mutual antagonism, couldn't you be the tactful third party?"

He sat and thoughtfully studied her face while drumming on the tabletop. "Your father would never believe I just happened by." Suddenly, Morgan's face lit up. "I have a date with you. How's that? If we're going to be sneaky let's do it up right. Your parents will think it's perfectly natural for me to drop by if you pave the way; tell 'em we have a date tonight. That'll take care of getting me in."

She nodded, but afterwards, as they were leaving the restaurant, a bad premonition came to disturb her. If, for example, her parents thought she and Morgan Harding had a date, wouldn't they also expect them to go out instead of linger at the house?

And there was something else: Undoubtedly acquaintances had seen her at the theatre with Morgan Harding, and she knew for a fact several people she knew had stared at them at the restaurant. This would be their third time together, and even if they stayed at her home for the evening, it wasn't impossible that neighbours would see his car parked out front.

Of course Arthur would understand. He'd said many times that jealousy was the exclusive prerogative of small, mean little people. Moreover, as soon as she could, she'd tell him how all this had occurred.

Nonetheless, by the time they parted at the kerbing, by the time Morgan rouguishly winked at her then turned and went buoyantly hiking towards the Larimore Building, her misgivings were beginning to pile up.

When she got back to the car and found her mother sitting behind the steering-wheel browsing through a magazine as she waited, she was tempted to confess the entire scheme and implore her mother to provide her with a way out.

She didn't though, and for the simple reason that she'd look awfully foolish since it had originally been her idea anyway, if she now telephoned Morgan to cry off.

Her final judgement was that she would go through with it, but the first chance she got afterwards she'd telephone Arthur and make a clean breast of it all. That thought comforted her through most of the ensuing afternoon. By early evening when her father arrived home, however, the misgivings were back as strong as ever.

She heard her father and mother discussing Grandfather Morris's forthcoming visit in the study, which was off the hall from her bedroom. Her mother was full of admonitory advice. Her father was his usual assertive self, but with reservations, as when he said, "I'm not going to argue with him, Alice. All I ever wanted was for him to keep his big beak out of our lives. Businesswise, I never crossed him. After all, he founded Morris and Morris; it was his business and I was simply the book-keeper. You understand. You said you did, at least, the night of the blow-up."

"Yes, sweetheart," purred Alice, dressed with more subdued elegance than usual in honour of this night. "I understand. But tonight, please be tactful. After all, he *is* an old man."

George grunted. "Humph! You make that sound like it's an excuse for Grandfather Morris to ride roughshod over people. Well — not here he doesn't."

"Just be diplomatic, George. That's all I ask. Anyway, maybe he's coming to patch things up. He didn't say."

"No, I can imagine he didn't. He'd just announce that he's coming over. Like De Gaulle. We're supposed to drop to our knees in grateful ecstasy. Well, I can tell you why he's coming. Morgan barged in on him and made him listen to Morgan's formula for bringing efficiency to Morris & Morris."

There was a long moment of silence, then Alice, sounding equally pleased and surprised, said, "He did? Whatever possessed him, George?"

Ellie's father laughed shortly and heartily. Evidently the idea of someone ramming something down Grandfather Morris's gullet pleased him no end. "Morgan's young, Alice, and has a pretty realistic philosophy; since he's got so little to lose he can afford to take risks. That sums it up, I think. In fact, although he's been working on the procedures for a month in his spare time, he didn't tell me a thing about it until he walked in the other day and said he'd been to see your father. The way he related it I almost dropped from the chair in astonishment, and yet it was hilarious, too. It seems your father threatened him with his cane and before Morgan left the old man made him have a glass of sherry wine with him."

Alice sounded mildly awed when she said, "George, this young man. . . . That was an awfully brash thing for him to do, wasn't it?"

Ellie could have predicted her father's reply. "Brash? I suppose so, Alice. But this is a brash world at times. I think the lad did a superb job of it."

Alice retreated. She knew very little about business in any case. "Well, all the same, dear, *do* be kind to Father tonight, won't you?"

Ellie finished dressing, finished making-up, then had to smile at her own reflection in the mirror as she visualised Morgan Harding confronting Grandfather Morris, the hard-hearted and strong-willed old millionaire patriarch, who sat there brandishing his cane. She could even imagine the epithets Grandfather Morris hurled at the younger man; she knew for a fact that in his early days her grandfather'd been a two-fisted, hot tempered, profane man. The temper and the profanity remained if the physical prowess had waned considerably over the past half century.

It must have been a fascinating confrontation. She also thought she knew something about Morgan Harding that not even her father knew; he could very forthright and hard-headed in his own right, when he wished to be.

Perhaps, Misgivings aside, this forthcoming meeting was going to be worth all the anxiety after all.

She gave her hair a final lick with the brush, stood for a quick glance in the full-length mirror, then hastened out to the kitchen where her mother was critically viewing the dinner she'd prepared for the three of them.

Alice looked, then slowly turned and looked again. "You look very regal," she said, raising her eyes to Ellie's face. "It's only your grandfather who's coming by, love."

Ellie teetered on the brink of making a confession, but at that moment her father came into the room, beamed on her and said, "My, you're the most beautiful female — barring one — I've ever seen. Alice, suppose we had a little highball before supper? I'm in the mood."

Ellie's opportunity to confess passed. As her father and mother collaborated in making a pair of martinis, Ellie took over the arranging of the food on plates. Once, standing beside the dining-room table, she glanced at the old Seth Thomas clock in the next room, saw that it was almost six, and felt her heart do a flip-flop in its dark place as the misgivings began crowding up again.

CHAPTER EIGHT

A SECRET IS NO LONGER A SECRET

Grandfather Morris was punctual. He'd often said it was his paramount virtue, the first half of his life, and the bane and exasperation of the second half, meaning, one was entitled to presume since he never explained *what* he meant, that in his sundown years he'd have preferred being lazy.

He looked fit for a man his age, lean, hawkish, testy, well dressed in loose tweed, which he'd always been addicted to, and if the shirt-collar hung loose, the tie was slightly askew, that was one of the beauties of tweed — you were never expected to look pre-eminent anyway.

Ellie helped the stiff-backed old man and her equally as awkwardly unrelenting father over the first few sentences, then Alice brought her father a small glass of wine — sherry, he was partial to it — and handed her husband another martini, very weak this time, and kissed Grandfather Morris's wrinkled old leathery cheek as she herded them both to the parlour.

"It's turning warm," she said, taking a seat and beaming on her father. "Seems a bit early for summer, doesn't it?"

Grandfather Morris peered from beneath

bushy, unkempt brows, eyes bright and sardonic. "Summer if always early, Alice. No one ever is really prepared when the heat arrives — unless they're as old and perennially chilly as I am."

"You should eat more, Father."

Grandfather Morris snorted and looked at George. "Eat more indeed. Two things women always bring up if you sit with 'em long enough: Food and babies. At seventy-two. I don't care a damn for either. Now then, George. . . ."

The doorbell rang. Alice looked up in mild surprise as Ellie whisked through on her way to the entry-hall. George and Grandfather Morris seemed not particularly concerned with this interruption, until Ellie returned, very pale but bravely smiling, and led Morgan Harding into the parlour.

"I meant to tell you, Mother, that Mister Harding and I had a date tonight."

Alice looked pleased but uncertain. George raised his brows at Morgan. It was Grandfather Morris who spoke, eventually.

"Well, what have you to say for yourself tonight, young man?"

It was his usual gruff greeting. Morgan smiled slightly at them all before returning the old man's stare and saying, "It's nice seeing you again, sir."

Grandfather Morris turned a fishy eye on his son-in-law. "He just happened to drop by, eh?" The sarcasm was as heavy as lead.

George blinked in surprise at this implication, then reddened. "You heard Ellie. They had a date. I knew nothing about it."

Alice seemed to crouch in her chair, ready to spring between her husband and father. But Morgan got into that breach first by saying, "What difference does that make, Mister Morris? Ellie and I'll be leaving anyway."

Grandfather Morris, looking half convinced, studied Harding dourly a moment, then said, "When we talked before, young man, you mentioned a tally-inventory; all right, we used that system once at the warehouse and the store. It failed because, as I neglected to tell you the other day, people just didn't bother toting up what was added and what should have been subtracted as merchandise was moved. Now then, you said the other day, if this system were delegated to one person, and if it were tied to the accounting office, the company would have an accurate running inventory, and financial balance sheet, day by day."

Morgan nodded. "Yes, sir."

"Well," added Grandfather Morris, "I've been thinking of what else you said. If these functions were handled by an outside book-keeping service it would cost Morris and Morris less than our current routine. How, I'd like to know, can that be?"

Morgan's answer was brisk. "Sir, under the Jarrett system we would —"

"The *Jarrett* system," growled the old man.

Morgan retained his smile. "The Jarrett system, sir. I'm a Jarrett Company employee. It's our system. Of course, if it means all that to you I suppose Mister Jarrett might entertain a suggestion to change it to the Morris system."

Grandfather Morris scowled. "The hell with the name. Call it whatever you like. Just explain one thing to me — how can a system that failed with Morris & Morris be made to work for less cost with increased efficiency."

"Our system, sir, would entail just one full-time employee — a Jarrett employee — at your establishment. His sole job would be to keep all inventory records. He would keep those records from day to day. He will send certified copies to our office in the Larimore Building at the close of each working day, and we will make the computations the next morning, so that any time you or your executives desire, you can telephone Jarrett Company and get your complete inventory and financial statement one day old."

"All right. And just how can you do all this cheaper than Morris & Morris can, young man?"

"Because, sir, as I've explained before, we'll only have one full-time employee where you'd have at least four. Maybe more. As for the accounting, it would be done in our offices, in conjunction with other similar accounts, the cost spread around — amortised, Mister Morris."

Grandfather Morris gestured for Morgan, who had been standing during this time, to be seated. He nodded and obeyed, leaving Ellie alone in the doorway. She and her mother exchanged a glance, then Alice rose, excused herself and headed for the kitchen with Ellie following.

George watched his wife and daughter leave the room, then thoughtfully tugged at the lobe of his ear. He was not normally a suspicious man, but right at this moment he appeared to be struggling with some kind of idea that none of this was quite as accidental as it was designed to look.

"And," said Grandfather Morris, speaking again, "what kind of cost-estimate have you worked on this — this *Jarrett* system of yours, Mister Harding?"

"We haven't worked any out, Mister Morris. We haven't been encouraged by you to believe you'd let us make the proper studies."

"What will these damned studies cost me?"

"Nothing," said Morgan, and Ellie's father looked at him sharply but did not interrupt. "We can make the studies, bring all the papers for your consideration within a week, and if you don't approve there'll be no charge. All we ask is good faith on your part, sir."

Grandfather Morris turned his bright, faded eyes upon his son-in-law. "George . . . ?"

Ellie's father spread both hands in an attitude of agreement. "Just as Mister Harding says. We'll do the work, you can like it or lump it. I mean, you can have Michael and Carleton look it all over and help you decide."

Grandfather Morris eased back in his chair, touched fingertips together and spent a moment studying Morgan Harding. Finally he said, "Well, if you're going to take Heloise out, don't sit over

78

there making her wait, Mister Harding."

"I'll sit, sir, and she'll wait," said Harding quietly, "until you give me an answer."

"What!"

"Look, Mister Morris, there are seven large mercantile establishments in Windsor. I mean, with Mister Jarrett's approval, to take this identical plan to each one. But I don't want to tackle all seven simultaneously. Our plan is delicate and will require a lot of study and work. I'll get the answers one at a time."

"I see. Starting with Morris & Morris."

"Yes, sir."

Grandfather Morris continued to press fingertip together and intently study Morgan Harding as he said, "All right, young man. Make your study. Don't try to bill me for it later; I'll tell my son the initial work is gratis." Grandfather Morris now waved one thin hand. "Now go and get Ellie and if she's mad at you I won't blame her."

Morgan rose, nodded and walked towards the dining-room, beyond which was the kitchen, where Alice and her daughter had retreated.

Grandfather Morris was silent, watching Harding leave, but as soon as he was beyond sight the old man leaned and scowled at his son-in-law. "George, what I came round tonight for was to suggest that you come back to Morris & Morris. Of course, you'd be head book-keeper now, with a corresponding rise in salary."

George sat in silence. The two men studied one another for a moment. Grandfather Morris finally sank back again. He knew his answer before he'd got it. In fact, it didn't look as though George was even going to give him a reply.

He said, "All right. I've been keeping informed. I know you've got most of the worthwhile accounts round town. Well, good for you. Carleton doesn't like it, but that's not too important. I'm still boss around here. All right, George; let your Mister Harding make his study, and I'll buy the service. But you two had better produce."

George's impassivity melted. "We'll produce, Mister Morris. We both have a real stake in making this work."

"George . . . ?"

"Yes, sir?"

"I'm glad to see Ellie is going out with a businessman."

George Jarrett's smile winked out. "She's not. That is, to my knowledge they've only dated twice. There's nothing to it, I'm sure."

"Too bad. By the way, that Cartier chap and some New York friends of his visited the bank this morning looking for a fifty thousand dollar loan. It was refused, of course."

George knew nothing of this, but he could have predicted the appeal would be refused. Grandfather Morris owned seventy per cent of the stock in the Windsor Savings Bank.

"Arthur Cartier inherited that much, Mister Morris. He must have some pretty big scheme in mind to need that much more."

"He has. He's ploughing his money, and as

much more as he can borrow, into some stage play that this friend of his will produce in New York. Cartier will be leaving Windsor in a few days. His friend left this afternoon."

"You are quite well informed," said George, drily, and the older man swung to glare.

"If *you* won't take an interest, then I have to."

"Why should *either* of us do it, Mister Morris?" demanded George, getting angry. "What business is it of ours?"

"Because, confound it, Ellie is planning to go with him. That's why."

"Ridiculous," growled George, shifting position in his chair. "They're only engaged."

"Rot," spat Grandfather Morris. "They are *not* engaged. Ellie's been hinting they are round town, but Cartier denies it. For your information, George, he does not plan to marry Ellie, although he *does* plan on taking her to New York with him." As George Jarrett's face reddened anew, old Grandfather Morris raised a hand for silence, and spoke on.

"Cartier knows I'm rich and that your daughter is my only grand-daughter. He knows that if she gets in straits in New York and wires home, she'll get money. I *told* you Cartier was no good. I've known a lot of actors in my time, George, whether you believe that or not, and I've yet to meet one that wasn't an egotistical, unethical, immoral scoundrel."

George almost broke in this time, but again the old man's hand rose warding off the interruption. This time it was knotted into a skinny old fist.

"And there's something else you'd better know. You *and* Alice. When Cartier got turned down at the bank he went to see John Forrest."

Old Morris paused, either to let that sink in as though it had great significance, or else to catch his breath. Then he leaned and spat the next words.

"Forrest called the bank, George, to make arrangement to transfer fifty thousand from his account to Cartier's account. Doesn't that strike you as a little odd?"

It did. George said, "John Forrest is a highly successful attorney. He wouldn't throw away that kind of money, Mister Morris. Sure it surprises me, but if he thinks —"

"Wait a minute," growled the old man, looking sardonically annoyed. "Wait a damned minute, George. Forrest has his reason for lending Cartier that money."

"What is it?"

"Your daughter's alleged fiancé, Arthur Cartier, has become officially engaged to Jane Forrest, the attorney's daughter."

George slowly sank back in his chair staring at his father-in-law. "I don't believe it."

"You don't have to. It happens to be true. You and Alice and I don't have to believe it. I'm thinking of Ellie. What will she think; how will *she* feel?"

CHAPTER NINE

THE BLOW FALLS!

As Ellie and Morgan Harding slipped out the back door, abetted by Ellie's mother, they could still hear the two men in the parlour. The last distinguishable words were: "I don't believe it!" and seemed to come from Ellie's father. Morgan rushed her along to the car, pushed her in and as he slid in beside her, said, "It went off too smoothly."

Ellie had to concur. In fact, she hadn't considered it probable they'd actually *go* on a date at all. In fact, this was something she'd made up her mind earlier in the day that must not happen again.

But it *was* happening. Morgan drove away from out front of the house looking quite pleased with himself. She was confident he had no idea how she really felt. Also, she had no intention of letting him know.

He drove up towards the theatre a little hopefully, but when she was only lukewarm to his hint, he headed on through towards the northward environs where there was a bowling alley. She shrank from the noise, the brilliant lights outside as well as inside the great building, and the crowd.

What she was seeking to avoid now was being seen in Morgan Harding's company *again*. Simple arithmetic indicated that the more often she went out with Morgan, the surer she was of being seen by Arthur himself, or by someone who would rush and tell him she was two-timing him.

It no longer did any good, telling herself he would understand and she could explain, because she knew, when she was honest with herself about it, that Arthur's ego was so great that he couldn't stand the idea of any other man ever taking out some girl Arthur was interested in.

The car halted, Morgan Harding turned towards her with one arm thrown up along the back of the seat, and said, "Listen, the only thing I was supposed to do was keep your father and grandfather from having a go at one another. I think I accomplished that, but to be perfectly frank with you, when I walked in they looked like they were getting along rather well without me. But still, that was my part and I played it. Now you're acting like I'm afflicted with some communicable variety of poisonous ivy, and I damned well resent that."

She raised soft eyes to him. "I'm sorry, Morgan. I don't mean to be such a wet blanket, but actually you see, I just didn't plan any further ahead than you intervening in the parlour."

"Which turned out not to be needed."

"Perhaps. But who could know that in advance?" She looked out the windscreen, they were parked near the edge of Windsor with the old cemetery across the fields, barely visible in moonlight, and off on her right was the little town-supported Community Park — called "the green".

"I think you probably tipped the scales. They hadn't been together long enough before you arrived for anyone to know what might have happened. Your arrival set the course, afterwards." She looked back at him. "You were needed."

"But not now, I'm not."

She looked out the window again, towards the green. "Let's walk a bit," she said, and alighted from the car without awaiting his reply.

He joined her on the far side of the car and peered out where grass and trees sloped away easterly. "In the early days," she said, enlightening him, "this was where people grazed their milk cows and sheep. The village green — a sort of community pasture. My grandfather used to tell me stories his grandfather told him about Indians trying to sneak up and run off a few sheep or a cow."

They strolled forward. It was a warm night with stars at arms-reach distance, with a filling-out moon beginning to make its light felt on earth. There wasn't a breath of wind stirring in the treetops, which was unusual for almost *any* New England night, and over where the picnic tables had been securely planted, upon deep-set fir logs into the earth, a small furry animal of some kind, intent upon burglarising a waste-bin, failed to detect their presence until they were quite close, then he whirled, looked at them once in frantic surprise, then hurled himself off the bin and went racing for some underbrush.

They laughed. Morgan said, "Raccoon. He got the fright of a lifetime. When I was a kid I had one for a pet. He was a chronic thief — socks, ties, belts, anything he could pack away and hide."

Ellie sat upon one side of the picnic table. Morgan sat opposite her. For a quiet moment they regarded one another, then he said, "Sorry, I forgot the cards." He seemed slightly embarrassed by their closeness as well as by her silence.

She took a deep breath and said, "Being very honest, Morgan, which may surprise you, I like you very much. You are very easy to be with."

His smile was crooked. "But your heart belongs to Romeo. Sorry, I shouldn't have said it like that."

"Morgan, you don't *know* Arthur."

He waved a hand in weary resignation. "No point in going over all that ground again, Ellie."

She watched him a moment, then leaned and said, "Tell me your honest opinion."

"No. I already have, anyway. You got mad. I'd as soon avoid that again, if possible."

"If I promise not to be angry?"

"Look, Ellie, if you're fond of a man and someone else puts him down, you're going to be indignant. That is, *if* you are really and truly fond of him."

She didn't dispute this because she knew it was true, but she had in mind that remark her grandfather had once made about women not understanding men. She was certain her grandfather had been wrong, but she wanted Morgan Harding's opinion of Arthur in order to prove this to herself.

But for a while it didn't look like he was going to give her his opinion. After he'd fenced with her, trying to half-heartedly change the subject, she said, "Morgan, friendship isn't just a lot of cotton candy. If you'd asked for candour in me I'd have given it."

He sat perfectly still gazing across at her for a moment before he said, "Okay, pet. I'll test your candour: Are you really in love with Arthur Cartier?"

She formed the word "yes" with her lips, but for some reason hung fire over uttering it for several seconds, and he blew out a big breath, looked saturninely at her and said, "Where there is hesitancy there is doubt. Okay, I'll tell you something."

But he didn't. He fidgeted on the bench, looked down across the greensward a moment as though organising his thoughts or formulating sentences, then he turned back and somewhat grimly plunged ahead.

"Your Arthur Cartier, Ellie, was engaged today to a girl named Jane Forrest."

She slowly reached with both hands to grip the edge of the table, stone-silent and stricken. He looked away before speaking again.

"I was in the bank today and heard a couple of people talking about it."

"It's just not true, Morgan."

He raised a hand. "Wait. Let me finish. I didn't think it was true either. After all, we discussed gossip in small towns, didn't we? So, I went for lunch up to The Purple Happening." Morgan's night-shadowed face turned bitter. "It's true all right. There were enough people up there laughing about it to convince me. And — there was this dark girl up there flashing a big engagement ring. I'd seen her a time or two before but until I asked a waitress her name. . . ."

"Jane Forrest?"

He nodded, reached impulsively to cover one of her hands with his hand, and for a moment had no more to say.

Overhead, the top-heavy moon rode across the sparkling heavens through shoals of brilliant stars, there was still no wind, and time seemed frozen. Tree shadows on the grass were soft and fat and wedge-shaped, that raccoon was silent in his secret place or else he'd fled altogether, but in either case he no longer figured in the world of the girl and the man.

She drew her fingers from beneath his hand. "Why? Why would Arthur do such a thing, Morgan? He told me he loved me. He said as soon as he got round to it he'd get the engagement ring."

"Love? Cartier loves only one person on this

earth and it's not you *nor* Jane Forrest."

She sprang up and turned to run blindly off down through night-shadows. He also sprang up, then he slowly sat down, studied his hands on top of the table for a bit, and after a while he simply slumped forward, leaning on the table, waiting.

It was a long wait. He could be that patient because he had no answers for any of the questions she'd ask, nor for the matter of that, not very many answers to his own questions.

Then he saw her, moving slowly, almost as though she were floating, down where the park sloped away among tall trees. She was strolling with an almost unearthly quiet. He rose to go meet her, but even when he was close she seemed neither to hear nor see him.

Not many men understand what emotional implosions do to women; Morgan Harding certainly didn't know. But common sense told him to walk behind her a discreet distance, keep her in sight, and that is what he did.

She turned, eventually, watched him approaching through tree shadows, and when he was near she said, "I've got to see him, Morgan."

He nodded, believing this was true, but what she said next stopped him in his tracks.

"I've got to see him now, tonight. Will you take me back to town and help me find him?"

He considered. "Let it wait until morning, Ellie. There's no telling where he'd be now anyway — is there?"

Her bitterness came through when she answered. "I think there is. I think we can find him." She turned back. "Are you coming?"

He went mutely along at her side beginning to regret telling her the truth about her handsome hero, at least this night, when, if they'd waited until morning, finding Cartier would be much simpler.

In the back of his mind was a premonition; engaged couples usually celebrated their plighted troth at someone's house. Perhaps, in this instance, at the girl's house. He had a vision of taking Ellie to the Forrest residence and having to stand by while there was a nasty scene.

As he held the car door for her he tried one last time to dissuade her. "Ellie, listen to me. Think about it over night. Make your mind up whether it's worth a confrontation or not."

She raised darkened eyes and said, "Don't worry, Morgan, I'm not going to embarrass you. All I want from him is one word. That's all."

He went round to his side of the car, slid in and somewhat tartly said, "You can use a telephone for that."

But he drove back towards town reconciled to whatever unpleasantness lay ahead, glum and irritated with himself. "Where would he be? At his hotel? Listen, Ellie, it's only going to complicate things having me stand around. . . ."

"You don't have to say it if you'd rather not, Morgan."

"Well. But how will you get home?"

"Someone . . . I can get a taxi, perhaps."

"This late? It's past ten o'clock. Ellie, suppose I take you directly home and in the morning we can go —"

"I want my answer tonight, Morgan." She turned, tense, big-eyed, distraught. "I shouldn't put you through all this. Morgan, just let me off somewhere uptown and I'll find someone who'll either take me round, or else I may be able to hire a car."

"Nonsense," he exclaimed, gripped the wheel with bleak conviction and kept on driving. "We'll try the hotel first."

"He won't be at his room."

"Where then?"

"At Jane Forrest's house. Take the second road on your left after we get past the Lee Building. I'll show you."

Windsor was half light, half dark. Most people were either already abed or preparing to be there. One of the town's three black-and-white police sedans was idling at the kerbing near the hotel. Its pair of uniformed officers eyed Morgan's car without much interest, and when he came on past the patrol car, made a wide U-turn and went slowly cruising back in the opposite, or northward, direction.

"There," said Ellie, leaning to point where a dark intersection loomed. "Turn left."

He obeyed, left the business section behind, and the farther along he drove the more expensive the homes became, the broader the lawns, the more quietly sedate and exclusive the looks of the neighbourhood.

"That house," she said, leaning towards him to indicate a lighted mansion on their left. "That's where the Forrests live."

CHAPTER TEN

THE STORM AND TUMULT

Despite the lateness of the hour there was undeniably some kind of celebration in progress at the Forrest residence.

Also, with the large house on top of a low grassy eminence so that observers were required to remain below and look up at it, back some little distance lending the place an air of exclusiveness, it was almost inevitable that newcomers should feel slightly diffident before ever turning up the driveway.

Possibly seeking clarification, Morgan said, "If I recall correctly, someone said Forrest is an attorney."

Ellie nodded, not looking away from the house. "He is. The most successful one in town. I've heard my father say many times that John Forrest would be his choice if he ever got into serious trouble and needed competent defence."

Morgan halted the car midway up the drive, turned and looked hard at Ellie. "In another few minutes there'll be no turning back," he said.

She slumped against the seat, gazing on past, up where light and noise kept the night from making its dark influence felt. It took a bit for her to find the words with which to reply, but ultimately she did.

"I thought — it was too late for both of us to turn back. For Arthur and for me." She made a ghastly little smile. "Of course, you're right, Morgan. I shouldn't walk in up there uninvited and confront Arthur, should I?"

He didn't reply but he slid the car into reverse and began to slowly back down the way they'd formerly driven up. He reached the street and swung to get clear just as another vehicle came up, blocking his access. Someone in that second car must have recognised Ellie because a girl's musical voice called her name.

Morgan growled something uncomplimentary under his breath over this delay, slid his car out of gear and waited almost stoically for the other driver to move.

She didn't move at all, instead, woman-like, she left her motor idling, left her car back there to block Morgan's withdrawal, and ran up to Ellie's side of the car to say, "I thought that was you, Ellie, when the car lights fell across the occupants of the car. Have you been up there? It's supposed to be quite a bash. I'm late as the devil," the girl laughed. "You know me; that's the story of my life."

"We weren't invited," said Ellie.

The other girl's face, still bravely clinging to its little smile, showed by the soft and sympathetic glance of the girl's eyes that she would perhaps have said more, would have touched upon something that lay heavily between them, except that inhibitions kept her from it.

"It's an — engagement celebration, isn't it?" Ellie asked.

The other girl said, "Well, no, not exactly. That is, there's been no official announcement as yet, Ellie. The party is really to help celebrate Arthur's off-Broadway production, shortly to be released, as they say."

Ellie smiled. "I don't want to hold you up, Carol. If you'll move your car we'll pull away and you can drive on up."

Carol said, "Sure." She was no longer smiling. "I didn't know you'd heard about the engagement, Ellie. I knew of course that you *would* in time, but not so soon. Well, I'd better move the car, hadn't I?"

After Carol had gone Ellie looked around. "I didn't behave very well, did I? It wasn't that I forgot to introduce you, it was rather that I didn't want to drag you into my troubles."

As Carol backed off and Morgan could swing clear, he said, "A little late for that, duck. I would hazard a guess that your friend Carol will drive up there bursting with the electrifying news that Ellie Jarrett was out here with some man. She may even embellish it." He straightened out the car and sent it hastening ahead. It was now past eleven o'clock and except for a few residences, a few night lights eerily glowing in stores as they resumed their way through the business section, Windsor was mercifully blacked out.

He turned once, smiling, and said, "You could

faint. I believe that's what all proper young ladies did about the turn of the century. Or you could rush to your bedside, fall upon your knees and take an oath to enter a convent and devote the rest of your pitiful existence to the service of the poor and deprived."

She looked at him, annoyed, but did not comment.

By the time they reached the kerbing outside her home she'd begun to return to rationality. A glance up at the house showed it to be dark and silent. She said, "Would you care to come in for a cup of coffee?"

He declined. "No thanks. I've had about all the stimulants I need for one night. Ellie . . . ?"

"Yes."

"I'm sorry I was the one who told you."

"I'm not, Morgan. And I'm glad it came tonight instead of tomorrow."

He didn't ask her reason for that, but he said, "Sooner or later you'd have been told, along with your parents."

She nodded glumly. "A while ago, offering me alternatives, you left one out: I can pack up and leave Windsor."

"I didn't overlook that, duck. It was too apparent to mention. No one ever has to point a coward's way out to a coward."

She stiffened, started to speak, changed her mind and got out of the car. He started to alight also but she told him she'd find the front door without his help. Then she leaned and said,

"Everything turned out different for both of us tonight, didn't it? I should say I'm sorry, Morgan, but I'm too numb to know exactly what I feel. Good-night."

"Good-night, Ellie. I'll drop around tomorrow."

She nodded, scarcely heeding, turned before he'd driven off and walked resolutely to the door. Inside the house there was the lingering fragrance of dinner, of coffee, of people. She went to her room, undressed in darkness and got into bed, where reflected moonlight made a pale streak across the ceiling.

She crumpled, finally, turned her face down into the pillow and wept.

The night was as long as only such nights can be. It had vague effigies and half-recalled snatches of things Arthur had said to her.

It also had the less sympathetic things others, such as Grandfather Morris, had said, not only *to* her but most certainly *about* her, about Arthur, about love and life, sadness and happiness, about all the things that inevitably befall people, maturing girls included. And the sum total of it all was bitter truth and physical exhaustion.

She slept like the dead. Not even a new day burnished golden with a fresh, huge rising sun awakened her. Alice came ultimately to rap softly on the door and call.

"Breakfast, Ellie. And there was a telephone call."

She rose, bathed, scrubbed her face first in

warm, then in cold, water, and expecting to find herself bruised in spirit, found instead that she was ravenously hungry, which was not exactly the proper mood for a girl whose heart had been smashed to pieces.

By the time she got to the kitchen her mother had cleared the dining-room table, had set Ellie's breakfast on the kitchen table so that, while her daughter ate, the mother was close by at the draining board, handy for conversation.

Alice was obviously sympathetic, which meant she somehow knew, too. Ellie was irritated, wondering if she'd been the last to find out. She said, "Mother, Arthur has become engaged to Jane Forrest." Then she waited for her mother to turn away from the sink with troubled gaze.

Alice did exactly that. "I know, child. Your grandfather told us last night."

Ellie was surprised. "Grandfather? How would he know?"

"Very little happens in town he *doesn't* know as soon as it happens."

Ellie began to feel the humiliation which was inevitable. "And he was grim about it," she predicted, but her mother dispelled that.

"No. . . . Well, you know how Grandfather Morris is, Ellie. Very outspoken and rational. He said you deserved it."

Ellie flinched. "Deserved it? I didn't even know it was going to happen."

"Yes, I realise that, Ellie. What your grandfather meant was that you deserved it for putting so much faith in a man who has no honour and no principles."

Anger made Ellie spring to Arthur's defence. It was an automatic reflex; she'd been defending him against people ever since she'd known him. "How can grandfather say such a thing, he doesn't know Arthur." There was more, but Ellie, remembering something the old man had said, checked herself.

Alice came to the table with a cup of coffee, sat and looked sadly at her lovely daughter. "I've taken your father's side against Grandfather Morris, child, and I would take your side, too — if I thought you were right."

"You don't think I've ever been right about Arthur, do you Mother; neither has Dad."

"For myself, child, I've *hoped* for the best."

Ellie saw the sympathy in her mother's eyes and softened. "I know, Mother. And I appreciate your faith in me. But I've been very wrong."

Alice was startled and showed it. "Wrong, child . . . ?"

"Wrong, Mother. I lay awake last night going over everything time after time. It wasn't losing Arthur that broke me up, Mother. It was realising that I was wrong about him, everyone else was right, and now I've got to face the consequences. I'll meet friends who'll be saying one thing and thinking another thing."

"You could go down to the city for a few weeks, Ellie. Go and do some shopping. There's nothing that does as much for a woman's inner self as new clothes, a fresh flirtation or two." Alice hastily raised her cup and drank, avoiding her daughter's glance.

Ellie did not make an issue of that last suggestion. She scarcely heeded it, in fact, because working out her own observation was uppermost. She began to pick at the breakfast Alice had put in front of her.

Finally, she said, "Who called?"

She thought she knew the answer and she was correct. "Mister Harding, child. He called shortly after your father had left the house. I told him I'd tell you, but I didn't promise you'd call back."

"He was being solicitous, Mother."

"That's very sweet of him."

"He's the one who told me, last night."

"I see." Alice picked up the cup and finished her coffee. She was non-committal about Ellie's last statement, as though unwilling to approve or disapprove of it until she knew what the full ramifications might be.

"I insisted on hunting Arthur down last night and facing him. Morgan talked me out of it. He said I'll be a lot wiser to sleep on it."

"That was excellent advice, Ellie."

"Maybe. I suppose it was. But I'm afraid I wasn't altogether logical last night, Mother." Ellie rose, took her dishes to the sink and started to wash them. "I'll call him back, of course. By the way, did Grandfather Morris agree to try Morgan's inventory-audit system?"

"Yes."

"Did he and father have an argument after we left?"

Alice brought her empty coffee cup to the sink and quietly said, "No, there was no argument. But your grandfather was upset over John Forrest lending Arthur fifty thousand dollars for the Broadway production."

Ellie turned slowly and stared. "Jane's father did *that?*"

"Yes. Arthur tried first at the bank, but you know that no one in Windsor would invest in a play to be produced in New York. So — Mister Forrest put up the money."

Ellie's eyes stung but no tears showed as she said, "Mister Forrest *bought* him for Jane?" Her lips trembled and when Alice was afraid Ellie was going to break into tears, she threw back her head and laughed. Then she spun away from the sink and ran back to her bedroom leaving Alice torn between a mother's desire to run after her, to share her anguish and to offer grieving sympathy, or to wisely remain where she was, finish the breakfast dishes, and let the storm run its course.

Alice decided on the latter course.

A little later George called, and Alice told him what had happened. He sounded choked with frustration and wrath but Alice told him that in her opinion the best either of them could do right now, was nothing.

He vented his fury with profane denunciations, which Alice listened to with disapproval but without admonishing him because she understood, and later, when he'd calmed himself, she said, "I suggested a week or two in the city. Thought she might want to buy some new clothes, see the sights down there."

George agreed. "Fine, love. That's just right. Find out what it'll cost and I'll make out the cheque this evening when I get home."

"She won't go, George."

Jarrett was appalled. "She won't? Well...."

"Don't worry about things. You have enough on your mind. We'll have a highball when you get home, and talk a little. Good-bye now."

"Good-bye, Alice. By golly I've got to hand it to you; when you *have* to come through, you do it every time."

Alice was smiling radiantly as she put aside the telephone.

CHAPTER ELEVEN

THE CRISES ANEW

Ellie didn't go uptown that morning despite her previous convictions about facing people, primarily Arthur Cartier. Instead, she worked hard and steadily in the rear garden, which was already quite well tended since it was her mother's particular hobby, but on the other hand it was a large area so there was enough to keep her active.

Alice had work to do in the house and only came out briefly to sit and talk to Ellie, when the mail came. There was nothing very interesting, barring a letter from a relative up in New Hampshire saying the late frosts had come, as usual, and had killed all the fruit tree buds, which meant there would be very little fruit in late summer.

Later, after a quick shower and a change, Ellie agreed to go uptown shopping for her mother. She returned Morgan Harding's telephone call just before leaving the house, and he said he'd meet her in the coffee shop on the ground floor of the Larimore Building in exactly one hour for a cup of tea or a glass of milk.

She drove up through the commercial section, drove past The Purple Happening, where she felt excluded now, drove into the parking area behind the market where her mother had been trading ever since Ellie had been a baby, and entered with her head up, her jaw out-thrust, her eyes clear and challenging.

But no one acted one bit different than they'd ever acted. Two of the youthful male clerks mildly flirted as they always had, and the older clerk, a man who'd been two forms ahead of Ellie through secondary school and was always paternal toward her although he couldn't have been more than two or three years her senior, helped her make several selections and quietly poked fun at her, teasing in the fashion of someone harassing a younger sister.

Then Ellie rounded a laden shelf and came face to face with Carol, the girl who'd arrived late at the Forrest's party the night before. Carol blushed furiously, which probably meant the sight of Ellie had evoked some instant and uncomfortable recollections. Ellie, calm and cool, had the advantage and employed it.

"You don't look any the worse for wear, Carol. The party must have broken up early."

"Well, not exactly. But *I* broke up early. Ran out of petrol about one this morning. After all, I'm not someone's playgirl daughter. I've got to work. In fact, I'm on a late lunch-break right now, trying to catch up on the shopping I should have looked after yesterday."

"How was the party?"

Carol stood a moment gazing at Ellie, sober and thoughtful, then she said, "By the way, I didn't mention seeing you outside last night." Carol shrugged. "No point in giving them anything to talk about." Carol grinned, acting a little relieved. "They didn't need it anyway."

"Why not?"

"Oh, you know how those things are. They were all making up outlandish stories anyway."

"About me, Carol?"

"Not necessarily, Ellie. I heard a little about you, but not too much. Mostly, everyone was thrilled about Arthur's prediction." Carol pulled a wry face. "Jane didn't even come off too well, and it was her bash."

Ellie relaxed a little, trying to figure out what was simple kindness and what was the candid truth. She'd known Carol since schooldays, too; like the store-clerks, she'd known the characteristics most noteworthy. Carol had never been a liar, for instance. She'd always been a terrible flirt, she'd always shied away from participation, outdoor sports, but of all the things one remembered most, was the truthfulness.

Ellie smiled. "I owe someone an apology, Carol. That man I was with last night. . . ."

"I know, Ellie. He works for your father. The girls have noticed him." Carol rolled large eyes. "Tall, pretty smooth looking." Carol's eyes settled back upon Ellie in a narrowed, speculative expression. "By the way: Arthur knows."

"Is that so?"

"Look, Ellie, you can't keep showing up at places like the theatre, The Purple Happening, stores around town, and driving out with him in his car, without people talking."

It sounded a little like Carol was delivering a mild scolding. Ellie nodded; she had promised herself several times to call Arthur and explain. She hadn't, so whatever Arthur thought he was perhaps justified in thinking. But if that'd had anything at all to do with his affair with Jane Forrest. . . . Ellie could think back to little things — like Jane's fingers gliding through Arthur's hair that time — and she let the thought die, because palpably it hadn't had anything to do with Arthur's sudden engagement at all.

She could have put a name to what *had* had something to do with the engagement — the Forrest fifty thousand dollars — and there were definite names for men who became engaged to daughters of men advancing them money.

Carol broke across Ellie's reveries. "I've got to finish up and get home. Ellie, take care."

After Carol departed Ellie happened to glance up. There was a lighted wall-clock showing that at the precise moment she was standing where she was, Morgan Harding was waiting for her in the coffee shop at the Larimore Building.

She caught one of the clerks, pushed the remainder of her unfulfilled shopping list into his fist, urged him to finish making selections for her, promised to come back before closing time for the load, and ran outside to her car.

The clerk gazed after her, shrugged and went to work. There really was nothing at all startling in his business about women standing and talking and forgetting everything else, thus making themselves late. In fact, if something about like that didn't occur every day, he'd feel that the business was definitely failing.

Ellie reached the coffee shop slightly breathless. Morgan was having a cup of coffee at one of the wall booths and rose calmly as she slid in opposite him. "You must have finished first," he said, glancing over a shoulder. "I don't see any of the other sprinters in sight." As he sat he smiled. "Or was it some evil old lecher, instead of a foot-race?"

She ordered coffee when the waitress hovered, afterwards considered his solicitous manner, his kindly, prodding eyes, and decided he was acting droll because he didn't know how else to act.

She told him of her encounter with Carol. He was attentive without commenting. He had the look of a man who doesn't want to disagree with someone openly, but who nonetheless doesn't agree with their judgement, which in this case was Ellie's statement that she didn't believe Carol had, in fact, told anyone at the Forrest party about meeting them outside last night.

Tactfully, he said, "Of course, the fact is — it just doesn't matter. Cartier has made his choice, you've made your choice, and that's about the size of it."

"Except that no one else will believe he didn't jilt me. Including me!"

He grinned. "*I* don't believe it, Ellie. You

couldn't make *me* believe in a solid year of argument. You may have loved Cartier once, but you haven't truly loved him now for quite a while. As I told you, duck, you haven't been very honest with yourself. You felt *obligated* to say you loved him. You were honour-bound to defend him against your parents, your friends, even your own best judgement, but there wasn't much honesty in that." He kept looking at her with his gentle little grin. "As for feeling jilted or crushed, or whatever girls feel when they discover a snake is just a snake, you asked for it, you deluded yourself one hundred per cent, and, lover, as far as I'm concerned, by this morning you ought to know you had every bit of it coming to you."

She wasn't angered, but she could not quite avoid a feeling of irritability. "And you are the preacher sent to scourge me, Morgan?"

He laughed, tossed off the remains of his coffee and dropped a silver coin on their little table, preparatory to leaving her. "Nope. I'm only the damned fool who is in love with you. *Really* in love with you." He rose, winked, turned and lost himself in the crowded little room heading for the yonder side door leading back into the foyer of the Larimore Building.

She wasn't really terribly shocked. In matters of the heart men are usually transparent. But she remained at their little table a little longer thinking back to the other things he'd said, and in the end her conclusion was that Morgan Harding and Grandfather Morris should get along famously; they both had identically unsympathetic thoughts on some subjects.

She left the shop, went back for the groceries and drove home just in time to miss a gossipy friend of her mother's who was driving off as Ellie drove in.

Alice helped her to bring the groceries in without much conversation, which was unusual, and afterwards, as they were putting things away, Ellie stole a private look at her mother's profile and saw the tough set to her mother's soft, full lips. She sighed, turned fully and said, with resignation, "Out with it, Mother. What did Mrs Wilding have to say. . . . No doubt about Arthur and me."

"Well, not too much about you and Arthur, actually. But then she wouldn't dare, you see. Not to me at any rate. But she had something interesting to say about Jane and Arthur. They are to be married tomorrow." Alice turned an anxious face, forcing a smile. "Aren't wasting much time, are they?"

Ellie heard herself say, "No, but then he has a reason. He's supposed to be down in the city within the next day or so to begin casting his production and to begin rehearsals."

She turned her back on her mother and resumed putting away groceries. It was hard, despite what Morgan or *anyone* said, not to feel the wound.

Alice was quiet for a bit. After the groceries were all stored away she began making preparations for dinner. She told Ellie her father would be arriving home a bit early, that it might be a good idea to set the dining-room table now instead of waiting another hour.

The objective, Ellie felt, was to keep her occupied, keep her hands busy and her mind off the impending nuptials. Ellie was perfectly willing to go along with it, if that would placate her mother, but after the first shock, she found herself reflecting on what she knew of the personalities of the two people involved.

She wasn't being vindictive when she thought there was actually no compatibility between Arthur and Jane Forrest; she was simply recalling what she knew of them both.

Then the telephone rang, scattering her thoughts, and since she was nearest, she got there before her mother, picked up the instrument and skipped a heartbeat as Arthur's clear enunciation came down the line in its customary velvet way.

"Look, Ellie, I've simply *got* to see you. There is something you're entitled to hear just from me, and —"

"Arthur," she said quietly, and saw her mother's brows shoot up over by the kitchen door where Alice was still standing. "Arthur, you don't have to explain anything to me — *now*. The time for that would have been a week ago. Or even day before yesterday. But not today or tomorrow."

"I simply must, Ellie, and I'm absolutely going to. That's all there is to it. I won't have anything as serious as a genuine disagreement standing between us. I'll be over tonight."

"Arthur, that's not necessary at —"

The telephone was dead in her hand. She raised her eyes to Alice. "He hung up before I could tell him I didn't want to see him. Tonight or any other time."

"You mean — he's coming here tonight, Ellie?"

"That's what he said, Mother."

Alice was stripping off her apron. "I think this calls for strategy, Ellie. We can't have him show up here while your father's around. I know your father well enough to realise he just might strike Arthur."

"Mother . . . ?"

"Don't worry, love," said Alice, balling up the apron and turning back towards the kitchen. "We'll clear the table, put the food back into the fridge, then I'll change quickly and hurry down to meet your father as he leaves the office. I'll make him take me to dinner at one of the uptown places."

Alice winked with forced joviality and Ellie winked back in something like the same mood. The last thing she had expected this evening, and the last thing she wanted, was a visit from Arthur Cartier.

But she was going to get it regardless.

As her mother fled, Ellie dropped her glance to the telephone briefly, started away, then stopped, turned back and glanced at it for a longer, more thoughtful moment. Finally, she turned back and picked it up, dialling the Larimore Building, but not dialling her father's personal number.

CHAPTER TWELVE

PLAYING A PART?

Arthur, who had made jokes about conformists being punctual people, arrived only a few minutes before eight o'clock, which was usually the hour he'd pick when he'd had dates which Ellie, except that those other times he was more likely to arrive at nine or nine-thirty.

She was unprepared, far from enthusiastic, or even pleased to see him for old-times sake, but ready for just about anything she could imagine she'd have to say.

But he would stun her before the visit was over.

He was well groomed, his wavy hair shone with its customary sheen, his face, aquilinely handsome head-on or in profile, had been lightly talced. The beautiful violet eyes were full of dark distress as he tried to take both her hands the moment she'd closed the front door.

"Baby, I've been trying to get over here and —"

"Arthur," she interrupted. "Don't. Just don't tell lies."

He followed her as far as the parlour, and when she turned to sit, he moved to the closest chair. "Ellie, believe me I've been stricken over the delays that kept coming between us. I wanted to explain."

"There's no need," she said. "You might have telephoned about the engagement. It wouldn't have been the thing to do, but if you weren't man enough to face me and tell me, at least you could have telephoned."

He leaned, hands extended, looking very theatrical, very upset and distraught. He was a competent enough actor and she knew it. "Listen, baby — this engagement bit caught me flat-footed. I swear to you I didn't know it was going to be announced."

She stared at him. The large, violet eyes were dark with emotion. "Are you trying to tell me, Arthur, Jane Forrest did this all by herself?"

"The gospel truth, baby. I honestly didn't know a damned thing about it until yesterday afternoon. Oh, a couple of friends came by earlier in the day to share their bottle, and they kept drinking to my forthcoming marriage, but I didn't pay any attention. They were both half smashed, y'see. Then, Jane came over later on and told me about the party and invited me over. *That* was when she showed me that ring and told me the story. I was engaged to her."

"Arthur, this is absolutely preposterous. I don't believe a word of it!"

Ellie sprang up, walked to a front window and stood with her back to him gazing out where darkness lay in lighter puddles where the trees did not fling their shadows.

He crossed over, turned her lightly and held her arms. "I told you, Ellie, that's the gospel truth!"

She was torn between a wish to believe and a conviction that he was playing another part, that he was, for some reason she couldn't fathom, trying hard to get things back where they'd always been between them.

He would have kissed her but she averted her face at the last moment, without struggling, and he dropped his hands, stepping back a little as he said, "Ellie, how could you have such little faith in me?"

That irritated her. "Easily, Arthur," she flared out. "Because you let me become a laughing-stock."

"But I told you, Ellie, *I didn't know myself!*"

She was almost convinced. He *looked* so convincing. The curse of this dilemma was that, as a professional actor, when would she dare believe he was himself, and when would he be acting?

The answer that dropped into her mind was cruel. He would *always* be acting, telling the truth or deliberately prevaricating. Life with him would be an endless series of things like this. It was even possible he didn't actually know when he was acting, himself. Her heart hardened.

"Arthur," she said quietly, in full control, "I have no idea why you're doing this. Janie would be furious."

"Janie be damned," he said, turning pale and bringing up a dramatic fist for emphasis. "Janie crushed me last night with her announcement at the party. I was thunderstruck. I was stunned."

"Were you? Look, Arthur, you just told me she'd told you *before* the party. *That* would have been the time for you to be stunned — not several hours later. And don't tell me you weren't at the party, that you didn't have a good time."

"Baby, I was so miserable, I got drunk as a lord."

Carol hadn't mentioned any such thing, and Ellie knew Carol well enough to know that if he *had* got drunk she'd have said something about it.

"I got drunk," he reiterated, "and went home early. Left Jane's damned party and drove home before it was over."

"How early did you leave, Arthur?"

"I don't know. I told you, I was smashed to the gills. Probably before eleven o'clock. Look, Ellie, you've got to believe in me. You've got to have faith." He suddenly straightened up, striking a pose. "*I* have faith in *you;* have I said anything about you running around with that book-keeper or whatever he is — that *person* we met one time at The Purple Happening? Well, have I?"

She moved away from the window, back towards the chair she'd vacated. He followed, evidently believing she was wavering. Actually, she was being critical; it wouldn't be difficult to learn — from Carol or someone else who'd attended the party — if he'd left early in a funk. But that wasn't what puzzled her. Why was he saying all this; what motivated him to deny the engagement to Jane Forrest? There had to be a reason, and since he was no fool, there had to be a very *good* reason.

She sank down into the chair, looked up and said, "Arthur, what will Janie say — what will her *father* say — if I telephone out there and tell them you're here and that you've been swearing up and down you and she are not engaged?"

He turned, flung out an arm and rigidly pointed towards the hall telephone. "Go and call," he commanded.

"Arthur. . . ."

"I insist, Ellie! I absolutely insist that you go right now and tell Jane I'm *not* engaged to her and never was. Tell her she knows perfectly well it was all her idea, right from the start. That she deliberately tricked me."

He was *so* convincing, and yet, sitting calmly watching him, Ellie had a firm feeling that this was one of his better roles. He was the outraged hero, the put-upon man of honour, the scurrilously treated champion of decency and righteousness.

It could have convinced an audience without doubt, but Ellie *knew* him. He'd told her dozens of times, with a sneer, what he truly thought of middle-class morality and ethics. But now he stood there, pointing towards the telephone, handsome face set in stern lines, his entire bearing that of outraged decency, acting the part of the very middle-class hero which she knew he scorned.

On the other hand she hadn't a single doubt but that he meant her to go to the telephone and call Jane Forrest, and she couldn't comprehend that at all.

"You'll lose fifty thousand dollars, Arthur," she told him. "Mister Forrest will take back his money, then where will the play be?"

He dropped his arm and blinked at her. "Who told you he'd put up any money?"

"In a place like Windsor, no one puts up half that much money without it getting around." She smiled thinly. "I'm not the only one who knows. I don't suppose very many people aren't also saying that Mister Forrest bought you for Janie, with that money."

He blushed scarlet. "Ellie, I refused that money twice. He insisted. I told him specifically there were to be no strings attached if I accepted. He said he felt confident the show would be a smash-success, that he'd always wanted to put some money into a successful Broadway production. Upon that basis, and that basis alone, I took his money."

"Are you prepared to return it, Arthur?"

He drew up erect again. "First thing in the morning. In fact, I'd like to have you accompany me when I do so."

She thought she knew what he was doing; Saying that because he knew very well she'd shy away from accompanying him to John Forrest's office where there would surely be a scene.

She was tempted to agree to accompany him, but in the end she succumbed to what he expected. She shook her head. "No thanks. You can do that by yourself."

"All right. I'll march in there first thing in the morning, tell him I'm not for sale, and give him his cheque." He leaned a little, turning soft and wistful towards her. "Then I'll come back and we'll go for a drive in the country. All right?"

"Let me think on it," she said, rose and started for the front door. "Arthur, I'll call you at the hotel. I need some time."

He was undecided. He also seemed to suspect that she was trying to get rid of him, which she was, but not because he'd overwhelmed her, confused her, bruised her heart and wrung her soul as he believed, but because she had another caller about to arrive, and although she'd wanted them to come face-to-face in the parlour, now she did not want this at all.

She opened the door. "Good night, Arthur. I'll call in the morning."

He bent, reverently pecked her cheek, drew back with both her hands in his hands, and said very softly, "You are my only love, Ellie. My only true love." Then he was gone forth into the benign night, and she eased the door closed and leaned upon it. Was still leaning upon it when she heard his throaty little sports car make its snarling way off towards the uptown centre of town.

She returned to the parlour, sat thinking, trying to figure something out, and was no closer to a solution ten minutes later when the second car arrived out front, than she'd been while Arthur had been roiling her emotions, as he always had done, when he'd been in the parlour with her.

She went to the front door, opened it and stood in the frame of lightglow as Morgan Harding came striding along. When he smiled up at her she only nodded and moved aside. But he stood fast on the porch. "Too nice a night, duck. Come on out and close the door."

She obeyed, he whipped a hand from behind him, and held forth a delicate spray of roses and green fern. "I always keep one of these handy when I have evil intentions towards some beautiful woman."

Now she smiled, in spite of herself. "They're lovely, Morgan. I'll be right back." She went indoors to the kitchen, sought a vase, put them in it and left them on the drainboard to be taken, later, to the bedroom with her.

He was cocked back on a porch chair when she returned. He didn't actually rise but he seemed about to, until she waved away that little gallantry, then he said, "Thanks, I'm tired tonight."

"Why?"

"I spent the entire day like a squirrel in a wheel, setting up our system at your grandfather's warehouse and store. And I might as well confess to you that your Uncle Michael gets my nomination as the guy in Windsor most likely to wind up with a fat lip if he doesn't quit following me around with critical comments."

She laughed. "And Uncle Carleton . . . ?"

"Sceptical but quiet. He should have been an undertaker. He didn't even make any noise when he walked. But I'll give the devil his due; Uncle Carleton isn't biased. Uncle Michael is." He turned, grinned, ran an appreciative eye over her, then said, "Okay, pet; did Lochinvar show up?"

"He left about a half hour, ago, or less. Morgan, he said he was *not* engaged to Janie Forrest."

Morgan's easy grin faded. He seemed just as stunned by this as Ellie had been. Then he recovered, gave his head a hard shake and said, "Well, if he *isn't*, he's sure got this damned town and everyone in it, fooled. Jane Forrest has the ring, I saw it myself."

"He said it was all her doing; the ring, the party last night, all of it."

Morgan leaned his chair down off the wall of the house, screwed up his face in tough concentration, and for a silent long time stared out across the garden towards the distant roadway. Eventually he said, "There's something sable in the woodpile. There's *got* to be, Ellie. It just doesn't make any sense this way. Everyone knows they *are* engaged." He turned narrowed eyes. "What about the fifty thousand dollars?"

"He said Mister Forrest loaned him that because Mister Forrest has always secretly wanted to be involved in show business, and there were no strings attached at all."

Morgan gave a great snort. "Mister Forrest always wanted to . . . ? Ellie, Mister Forrest hasn't a venturesome nor romantic bone in his body. All you have to do is look at him; slit-eyed, pudgy, a bear-trap mouth." Morgan shook his head again, but this time with greater emphasis. "Give me a cup of coffee, then I'm going home to bed, love, and tomorrow morning I'll get to the bottom of this and telephone you."

She stood up, relieved, because if he hadn't volunteered she'd have asked him to do just exactly as he'd said. "Go on and get your coffee," she said, moving back towards the door again.

CHAPTER THIRTEEN

AN UNGENTLEMANLY ACT

By the time Ellie got to sleep that night her parents had returned. Alice opened the bedroom door to peek in and ascertain that Ellie was still awake, then she laughed softly.

"I ought to do that more often, Ellie. Your father not only took me to dinner, he also took me to the theatre. It was a jolly evening."

Alice stopped beside her daughter's bed. There was enough moonlight or starlight to make faces and figures discernible. She leaned a little to examine her daughter's face, then she said, "How was *your* evening?"

Ellie related all that had happened. Alice listened, as astonished as everyone else had been, and afterwards she said, "Well, I'm sure if anyone can find out what's behind it all, it will be Morgan Harding. Your father was telling me on the drive home how hard Mister Harding is working to make the Morris & Morris account permanently a Jarrett Company enterprise. He certainly seems to be a most unusual young man."

Alice bid her daughter good night, left the room, and ten minutes later Ellie was sound asleep. When she awakened after what had to be only a few minutes, it was dawn, the world was awakening, beyond a ragged series of sawtooths stood the fresh new sun, and an occasional car sped past out on the street.

She felt rested enough, but for a few luxuriously languid moments she lay abed thinking of nothing at all, giving her body that one last moment of relaxed pleasure.

Downstairs Alice had breakfast ready early because George had to be at the office early. He had more bounce to his step, more flash to his eye, more verve to his manner, since leaving Morris & Morris and establishing his own business. Also, and whether he was entirely aware of this or not, Alice most certainly was, his instant success had made the transition from a regular, secure weekly pay cheque to a much greater monthly participating dividend, delightfully pleasant, and *that* was not only very unusual but it was also wonderfully gratifying.

Now, with Morgan Harding working just as hard to build the business, Alice was confident of its success. In fact, when Ellie came into the kitchen for coffee and cereal, Alice said, "I've been thinking, love, your father and Mister Harding make such an unbeatable team it would be a shame if we were to lose the junior member."

Ellie started to say something, checked herself and stared at her mother. Finally she laughed. "If you're thinking I should rush up and snare Mister Harding, Mother, in order to ensure the permanence of the Jarrett Company, I must say you've become terribly mercenary lately."

Alice brought a cup of coffee to the table with her, sat opposite Ellie and, looking very serious, said, "He's fond of you, evidently, or he wouldn't be dropping by so often. And I'm confident he's much more dependable than Arthur." Alice offered Ellie a tentative smile. "You must like him, child, or you wouldn't depend upon him so much."

Ellie caught that one word and held it. Depend. She hadn't sought to define her relationship with Morgan Harding before; that is, she hadn't condensed it down to any one applicable word, but now, sitting there finishing breakfast, she thought her mother had inadvertently provided her with the correct word.

She depended upon Morgan; she relied upon his strength, his judgements — even the ones she liked the least — and she couldn't deny that except for him she'd have done some foolish things. But it took more than dependability, strength, sagacity, to make a woman yield.

Ellie said, "Mother, I don't love him."

Alice didn't so much as bat an eye as she said, "Could I get you another cup of coffee, child?"

"No thanks."

Alice went after a re-fill for herself, and with her back to the room she said, "That's only half the battle, duck," and although Ellie strove insistently to make her mother define what she'd meant by that remark, Alice never did.

Later, when the telephone rang, Ellie rushed to it expecting Morgan to be at the other end of the line. It was, instead, her mother's brother, Carleton Morris, asking briskly to speak to Alice.

Ellie returned to the kitchen, passed on the message and finished tidying up, then went out into the back garden where the summer sun was already at work drying dew, loosening buds, warming rich earth and heightening the blush of each rose, each bed of petunias, every other flower, of which there were many.

A half-grown puppy out adventuring trotted up the driveway, around the corner of the house, saw Ellie and turned to flee with both ears flopping. She laughed and the puppy may have interpreted that to mean she was about to start in pursuit, because with a little yelp he doubled speed and disappeared in a great rush.

It rarely took more than something like that to set a mood for the day. Ellie was still smiling when Alice, wearing her wide-brimmed gardening hat, came from the house. Ellie told her mother of the interlude and Alice smiled absentmindedly.

Ellie studied her face a moment, then said, "What's bothering you?"

"Well, as you know, that was your Uncle Carleton on the telephone."

"So. . . ."

"Well, he was trying to locate your father."

"Did he try the office?"

"Yes. He's not there."

"Why should that be so upsetting; surely you don't think Dad's out with some floozy."

"Ellie! Of course not!" Alice raised her head to peer from beneath the enormous brim of her gardening hat. "Mister Harding struck Michael this morning at the warehouse."

Ellie seemed to be struggling with a desire to laugh aloud. Alice peered at her, perplexed, then she assumed a stern expression.

"It's not very amusing, Ellie. That could ruin everything your father's been working towards, you know."

Ellie was remembering what Morgan had said the night before. "Uncle Michael had it coming, Mother. He's been heckling Morgan over the new inventory-audit system."

"Did Mister Harding tell you that?"

"Last night, love, on the front porch."

Alice promptly forgot the other affair and said, "I didn't know that."

Ellie scowled. "Mother, while you were in my bedroom last night I told you that after Arthur left Morgan drove up."

"Did you, dear? I'm sorry. I must have been thinking of something else. Well, in any case, it wasn't very dignified of Mister Harding to strike Michael."

"What did your brother say about it?"

"Understandably, he was outraged. He wanted your father to know that he was going to order a stop to the inventory-audit survey immediately, and that he is going to report the interlude to your grandfather."

Ellie fell silent for a while, turned to weeding

the flower bed nearest her, and for perhaps ten minutes she was preoccupied, then she rose, wiped her hands and strode purposefully towards the house.

Alice looked up but said nothing. As Ellie disappeared inside Alice shrugged slightly and went back to her own weeding, and worrying.

Ellie's concern was about equally divided between the affair of Morgan striking Michael Morris, and Morgan's failure to call her and explain what he'd found out about Arthur's new attitude. But she did not call Morgan, she telephoned her grandfather, and as soon as he came on the line she said, "This is Ellie; are you going to stop the inventory-audit study?"

Grandfather Morris hesitated for a moment, for although he was blunt himself, he seemed surprised to find that Ellie was also that way. Finally, he said, "Why do you ask, Heloise?"

"Because, Grandfather, I can tell you that Uncle Michael had it coming."

"Had what coming?"

Ellie's fervour suddenly collapsed. "Didn't Uncle Carleton call you?"

"Yes. I just finished talking with him."

"Didn't he tell you Morgan Harding struck Uncle Michael?"

"Yes." Grandfather Morris made a grunt, then said, "Oh, that. Of course I didn't order an end to the inventory-audit study just because someone knocked Michael down."

"You didn't?"

Grandfather Morris made a rare little chuckle. "Hells bells, girl, if I stopped everything every time in my life someone got knocked down, the entire seventy years would have been a series of starts and stops."

"But Uncle Carleton said —"

"I know what your uncle said, and I also know something else: Michael is an insufferable individual when he wants to be one. I told Carleton to keep that study moving along. I also told him to tell Michael that without knowing any of the details I'm inclined to believe he's lucky the young man didn't brain him, and if I hear any more of this schoolboy monkey business, I'll personally come down there and use my cane on Michael."

Ellie got a little lump in her throat. "I love you," she said, and rang off.

She was midway across the kitchen on her way back outside when the telephone rang, summoning her aback. This time she was sure it would be Morgan, but it wasn't, it was her father, and she knew from the noticeable edge to his voice that he wasn't in a very good humour. She told him Alice was out back in the garden, so he said, "Did Carleton call a bit ago?"

"He called. He told Mother about the affair between Uncle Michael and Morgan."

"Was she upset?"

"A little, yes."

"Well, you tell her everything is going to be all right," said George Jarrett, "and that damned brother of hers had no business telephoning and upsetting her. As soon as I can find Carleton, I mean to tell him hereafter to keep his complaints to himself if he can't locate me."

Ellie elfishly grinned. "Daddy, please don't strike him. One belligerent down at Jarrett Company is enough."

"Morgan," snarled her father, "is *not* a belligerent. I know what Michael's been doing ever since we started our survey at the warehouse. Morgan should have done it several days ago."

"Grandfather was of a similar opinion," said Ellie, and heard her father suck back a sharp breath.

"You've talked to your grandfather on this?" he asked.

"Only a few minutes ago. He said about what you've just said. He also told me he'd ordered the survey to be continued."

"Is that a fact? I haven't been able to reach him and I've been trying for the past half hour. You're quite sure of all this, Ellie?"

"Positive."

She detected the enormous relief in her father's tone of voice as he said, "That's very interesting. Well, tell your mother there's nothing to be upset about. Good-bye."

"Daddy, promise — no scene with Uncle Carleton?"

George's tone got testy again. "Of course there'll be no scene. Good-bye!"

Ellie lingered in the hall half-smiling to herself.

She lay a hand lightly upon the telephone, tempted to dial Morgan's number at the Larimore Building, but refrained, finally, because he obviously had enough on his mind at the moment.

She also remembered her promise to call Arthur at his hotel room, though, and even with the reluctance she felt about doing this, she had a good deal of curiosity prompting her fingers, so she dialled the number, half hoping he wouldn't answer, that he wouldn't be at the hotel this late in the morning.

She got her wish. The telephone rang and rang, no one picked it up, and, vindicated, Ellie broke that connection, heaved a big sigh and returned to the garden to explain to her mother all that had transpired since she'd gone indoors.

Alice was relieved, obviously, but she did not smile at Ellie's obvious amused attitude until Ellie related what Grandfather Morris had said about Michael being struck down. Even then, though, Alice's grin was weak and wavery.

"Very ungentlemanly though," she murmured. "I'm surprised at Mister Harding."

"You'd be more surprised, Mother, if you knew him better, and he *hadn't* done anything about being harassed."

Alice fixed her daughter with a shrewd-tender look. "Do you know him that well, Ellie?"

The answer was a slow look and a slow nod of the head. "I think I do, Mother."

Alice went back to her weeding, lost in her

private thoughts. The only clue to what she *might* have been thinking was the soft little ghost of a complacent smile down around her lips.

CHAPTER FOURTEEN

THE AFTERMATH OF UNPLEASANTNESS

Shortly before noon Ellie tried reaching Arthur again, had no luck, and tried one last time about an hour later. That time she hung up after five rings and pondered.

It was quite like Arthur to agree to be somewhere, then to blandly forget all about it. He'd told her any number of times with that scorning gesture he sometimes employed, that creative people were above the mundane details of everyday living.

But it was equally as probable that he was up to his armpits in trouble, if he'd kept his word and had given John Forrest's money back to the lawyer. That worried her a little. In fact, the longer she pondered, the more worried she became.

There was only one person she could turn to about all this. She hung back from calling Morgan until the strain was too much, then she waited until it was a little closer to the end of the day, when he'd more probably be in his office, and finally put in the call.

He was there, and he answered a little crisply, as though he were expecting someone towards whom he'd have to be defensive.

She said, "It's Ellie. I know you're terribly busy, Morgan, but I wondered. . . ."

"Ellie," he said, cutting across her words with a sudden freshness in his tone. "I was going to call you in a few minutes. Look, suppose we have dinner somewhere uptown tonight."

She shrank from that, instinctively. "Couldn't you just drop by like you did last night?"

"Well, if you'd like. But I've got quite a bit to tell you. This has been a very interesting day."

She knew what he was referring to, and almost commented on his altercation with Michael, but feminine intuition told her to say nothing, told her to let *him* tell *her,* since he evidently wished to, and since it would be much more tactful for her to simply listen. She already knew, from watching her mother, that a wise wife never interfered with the supremacy of the male.

She agreed to be ready to go to dinner with him at seven, and although she was bursting to ask what he'd found out about Arthur, she refrained. The art of being a woman, she told herself, was not the easiest role anyone ever had to play. For one thing, although she'd tried several times to reach Arthur, which was all she'd promised Arthur she would do, going to dinner with Morgan with an almost dead-certainty of being seen and recognised in his company, would not make things any easier between Ellie and Arthur.

But, she argued, *she* had done nothing to jeopardise that relationship with Arthur. Whatever had ensued *he* was responsible for. Furthermore, she did not believe all that he'd told her. She *had* to believe he was earnest about giving the money back to John Forrest because Arthur had made that the primary issue of their continuing relationship. By now, however, knowing he'd prevaricated otherwise, she was cynically sceptical of the reason why Arthur would return the money.

That, not the engagement to Janie Forrest, was what Ellie could not fathom yet. Also, that was what kept her dangling between some form of reinstated relationship with Arthur, and no relationship at all. In short, it was this doubtful but persevering feeling that Arthur just might possibly be sincere, that kept her hanging back from going to dinner with Morgan. From really sitting down and analysing her private feelings towards Morgan.

It was not a pleasant nor an easy dilemma.

As she told her mother she wouldn't be at home for dinner this night, and afterwards went to her room to get ready for the date, she hoped very much that Morgan would be able to explain everything. She had a feeling that even if he couldn't fulfill her wishes in that direction, at least he'd be able to set her mind somewhat at ease.

Then, lying in the bath, she thought of that word her mother had provided, and smiled crookedly. She was depending for an awful lot upon Morgan Harding.

But of course there was, as far as she could see, no actual connection between being dependent upon someone and being in love with them.

Ellie was not quite twenty, her vocabulary did not include the word "propinquity".

The day came to a slow ending, noticeably longer than days had been a few weeks back, and there was still birdsong when her father arrived at six o'clock. There was also a doubtful growl when Alice informed him that Ellie would be going out to dinner with Morgan Harding instead of eating at home with her parents.

"She hadn't better keep him out late. He had a tough day today."

When Ellie appeared, and kissed her father, he said the same thing again, but without the same gruffness. She promised not to keep Mister Harding out too late, and mischievously winked at her father.

"After all, for boxing one must be in shape."

It stung her father, as she'd teasingly intended for it to. He peered narrowly at her as Alice pushed a highball glass into his hand. "I wouldn't tease *him* about that little episode if I were you. He caught enough hell from me."

"I thought you weren't going to say anything to him, Dad."

"Ellie, I didn't tell you any such thing. I said I thought he was justified."

"Well, isn't that the same thing, Dad? Do you go about growling at people you approve of?"

"I don't want to discuss this," said her father.

"I've had nothing but this one subject all day long and I'm sick and tired of it!"

Alice turned. "Ellie, go into the parlour and wait for Mister Morgan." It was a quiet, soft command. It was the one tone of voice Alice had used with her daughter since Ellie had been able to walk, when Alice was displeased. It had always been enough.

Ellie smiled at them both. "You win. You two always win. I wouldn't have it any other way." She turned and left the kitchen with her father gazing quizzically after her.

He sipped the martini, smiled tiredly and said, "She's really quite a girl, Alice. She told her grandfather today that Morgan did exactly right in punching Michael. It tickled the old man."

"Did Father tell you, George?"

"No. I never got through to the old devil."

"George!"

He ignored the indignant admonition, finished the drink and kept right on smiling at his wife. "I talked to Carleton, though. Went over to his office and had a long talk with him. He was as mad as a scalded cat. He's the one who told me about Ellie calling your father. He also told me that regardless of what your father says in the future, if there's another outbreak of unpleasantness, he'll prohibit anyone from Jarrett Company stepping foot on Morris & Morris property."

Alice knew her brother, could visualise his very erect stance, his pinched-down features, his indignant glare. She said, "What actually happened between Mister Harding and Michael, George?"

If her husband felt exasperated at having to return to this subject he was weary of, he gave no sign of it as he stepped up to the highball mixer and poured his glass full again. "Mike's been heckling Morgan all week. He seemed to want to see Morgan's scheme fail the worst way. Yesterday he said, instead of the audit-inventory clerk being a Jarrett Company employee, he was going to insist the person be employed by Morris & Morris. This morning he started on that again. Morgan pointed out that an impartial service had to be managed by impartial people. Mike said Morgan was just trying to get a foot in the door at Morris & Morris, that Morgan wanted to move in himself. Mike called Morgan a liar when Morgan denied this allegation, and that was the end of the rope. Morgan knocked him flat."

"Was Michael hurt?"

"The indignity is all. Half a dozen Morris & Morris employees saw him lying flat on the floor."

"Was that all, George?"

"Just about. Mike got up, dazed, and took a big swing which Morgan ducked under, then Morgan grabbed him and held him with both arms to his sides, and told Mike to leave because if he didn't, Morgan was going to mop the floor with him. Mike rushed to his office and sounded the alarm; he tried to get your father, failed, and got Carleton. He even tried to reach me, but I was out of the office with a client."

"Did you see Michael at all, George?"

Jarrett sipped his martini with a thin smile up around his eyes. "Yeah. I waited until shortly before closing time then drove down to the store. I wanted Mike to have time for cooling down." Jarrett, still faintly amused, touched the slanting edge of his jaw. "There was a red spot right here, Alice, but that was all. Mike started screaming about being attacked. I laughed at him. I guess that wasn't very wise on my part, but he looked so ridiculous, standing there crying out about being attacked, and all he had was that little red place. Anyway, he got mad all over again. I told him he'd been asking for what he got; that if it'd been me I'd have done a damned sight more. Then I left and came home."

Alice, working over dinner, was discreetly silent for so long George finished his second drink before it dawned upon him she hadn't spoken. He said, "Well . . . ?"

Alice lifted her face and smiled. "Go and get washed for dinner, dear."

"Sure," muttered her husband, putting aside the empty glass. "What else have you got to say?"

"Nothing. As you say, Michael probably had it coming. Of course, we all wish it hadn't happened."

"I don't," snapped her husband, and stalked out of the room.

Alice waited until she heard a car stop out front before peeking round the dinning-room door to see if the newcomer was indeed Morgan Harding.

It was, and he looked freshly shaved and dressed, and actually quite handsome. She looked for some tell-tale mark on his face, found none, and decided everything had happened just about as her husband had said, then wiped both hands on her apron and went forth to smilingly welcome Harding.

She did that for a tactful reason. There would ordinarily have been no reason for her to barge in when a young man came calling on Ellie, but today things were different; she didn't want Morgan feeling that there was resentment against him over the awkward little episode at the warehouse.

She told him how nice he looked, told him all the splendid things Ellie's father had said about him, and then, when she could see how pleased and relaxed he was, Alice turned and winked at her daughter, then excused herself and departed.

Ellie understood. It was possible Morgan also understood, but neither of them said much until, driving away, he looked at Ellie with a little grin.

"She's terrific. If you could be like her. . . ."

Ellie was startled. "What do you mean, *if* — I *am* like her."

"No. Maybe some day, but not yet."

Ellie said, "I think I'm insulted," and they both laughed.

They had a mile or more to go before reaching the lighted centre of town. On the way he surprised her with a tactful remark.

"I reserved a table at a place just beyond the city limits. Not much point in going to one of those restaurants in the heart of town. I mean, we've got a lot to talk about, but apart from that there's not much point in having it taken back to Cartier that you're out with me again."

"He doesn't own me," she murmured, but without much conviction, and she *was* pleased that Morgan had been this considerate. Then she smiled at him. "Poor Uncle Michael. You ought to be ashamed of yourself, he's got to be at least fifteen years older than you are."

He grinned happily. "I'm ashamed just like I'd be ashamed about stomping on a snake that had just bit me. Terribly ashamed. Poor Uncle Michael indeed. Anyway, I heard today he's your cousin, not your uncle."

That was true. Michael Morris was the only son of Grandfather Morris's dead brother, but as far back as she could remember she'd always called him uncle; probably because he was so much older than she was.

"Old habit," she explained.

"Same here, Ellie. Old habit. When people keep picking on me, eventually I pick back. I'm only sorry he was your uncle — or cousin — or whatever he is."

"I'm not angry with you, Morgan."

"That's good. I had in mind making love to you tonight. It's never altogether successful if the girl's mad."

She looked at his profile with a stern flash of her eyes. "Don't bother. I've got enough problems already."

He turned, grinned slowly, and said, "Lady, when *I* make love to women, they *forget* all their other problems."

She responded to his teasing mood with a smile. "It's only your inherent Yankee modesty that keeps you from reiterating that."

He winked. "For a woman, you're fairly intelligent."

"For a change, Mister Harding, how would you like it if *I* slugged *you?*"

They laughed, and the evening got off to a good start. It usually did, as a matter of fact, when they'd got together lately. Not at first, true, but lately; in fact the more they were together, the more she had to admit he was fun to be with.

CHAPTER FIFTEEN

A CLANGER!

The place they ate was actually a kind of roadhouse. That is, a generation or so earlier it had been a speakeasy, a place where the daring residents of Windsor went for their illegal whisky. Since those times, with the repeal of Prohibition, it had become a tavern again, openly, but along with that, it had an excellent dining-room which was separate from the drinking rooms.

The speciality was barbecued beef, and it was delicious. Ellie had no idea that she was really hungry until the food was placed before her. Morgan admitted to a great hunger and proved it by eating at a great rate, with no intervening conversation for quite a while. Eventually, with the edge off his hunger, he said, "Windsor is a deceptive town, Ellie. I came up here convinced I'd find old-time New England — thrifty, prim, moral, unpretentious, God-fearing, and instead I find a phony arty café, a bunch of mixed-up young people, some hidebound merchants, and tremendous business opportunities."

"I'm so glad," she said ironically, "that you are quite taken with our town."

He grinned, let a waiter re-fill his coffee cup, and glanced round the shadowy room before turning back towards her and saying, "I'm taken with it, love. Only it doesn't quite square up to the New England image. For example — an attorney named Forrest exploded today, his daughter threatened to commit suicide, and our Hero, that most astounding actor Arthur Cartier, made a scene no one who saw it will ever forget."

Ellie put aside her fork. "Don't make jokes, Morgan. What really happened?"

"I just told you. And I've got to make a joke out of it, believe me, or it's just not believable. Arthur Cartier appeared in John Forrest's office this morning, flung down a certified cheque for fifty thousand dollars with a very dramatic flourish — if my informant is reliable, which I think she is — and —"

"*She* is . . . ?"

"It is Mister Forrest's secretary, duck. I met her the first week I went to work for your father. We occasionally have coffee at the downstairs shop together. Now please let me finish."

"I'm sorry. We'll get back to *her* later. Please go on."

"Cartier walked in, flung down the cheque, made a very dramatic flourish, then told Mister Forrest he did not want the money, that he was not going through with the engagement to Janie, and that he'd be leaving Windsor within the next couple of days. Seems to me, Ellie, he's been going to leave town for the past month, but he somehow never can quite tear himself away."

"He did it," she murmured. "I half thought he wasn't telling the truth last night when he said he'd give back the money."

"He was telling the truth all right, duck," said Morgan, bending to pick up the coffee cup. "What's fifty thousand greenbacks to someone who has that much in his own right, already?"

"But he needs more, Morgan. He told me he couldn't get the show open without at least that much."

Morgan sipped, nodded, and sipped again. "Righto. But he got it. In fact, little lady, he got *three times that much!*"

"What are you talking about? Are you saying Arthur got a hundred and fifty thousand dollars?"

"I am. I'm saying that." Morgan's blue gaze was stone-steady and sardonic. "He has enough now, including his own fifty thousand, to see his off-Broadway production through rehearsal, through its first fledgling weeks, and perhaps even enough to get it *on* Broadway, providing the damned thing's any good at all."

"But where? I'm sure he didn't get it from our local bank."

"You don't really want to know, Ellie, because if I give you the name of the person who put up that hundred and fifty thousand, you're going to put a few things together, and the sum you'll come up with will make you sick like it did me."

"I've *got* to know, Morgan."

"Why? Look, Cartier's going to get his money and he's going to pull out within a day or two.

Ellie, he's *not* going to come round and ask you to go with him."

"I understand that; he'll take Janie with him."

Morgan shook his head. "He's not going to take her either. He's going alone, and you can bet your boots he's going because that happens to be part of the stipulation involved in his acquiring the hundred and fifty thousand."

She looked at him with her eyes perfectly round. "Someone — *bought* him?"

"Yes, love, to put it in just a few words, someone has bought him. And love, there was never a more willing slave. Cartier would sell his heart and soul, providing he has a soul, for a lot less than a hundred and fifty thousand dollars. Take my word for that!"

"Who bought him, Morgan."

"Finish your dinner. It'll get cold."

"Morgan!"

He leaned back and did something she'd never seen him do before, he fished forth a pipe, fished out a pouch, carefully, almost solicitously packed the pipe, then lit it with a professional pipe-smoker's delicate care, and afterwards blew fragrant smoke ceilingward, clamped powerful teeth round the pipe-stem and said, "Your grandfather, Ellie."

It was like a heavy blow between the eyes. She blinked and rocked back slightly in the chair. He puffed a moment, removed the pipe, tamped its coals with a thumbpad, and nodded at her.

"If you'd like to know how I found that out,

I'll have to tell you it wasn't a very ethical method I employed. I had access to the Morris & Morris commercial accounts at the bank for the purpose of my inventory-audit survey. I got a naïve bank clerk to let me peek at Grandfather Morris's personal account. There it was — one hundred and fifty thousand dollars paid in a cashier's cheque to Mister Arthur Cartier, day before yesterday. I had in mind going out and looking Cartier up to verify this. In fact I was a little angry and indignant about that transaction, when Uncle Michael or Cousin Michael, or whatever he is, got loud and troublesome. I suppose you might even say that it was your fault I punched Michael. But, in any case, that caused such a flap I never got round to looking Cartier up. But Ellie, it doesn't matter. Now, after all day to think about it, I don't want to see Cartier. I don't even want to be where he is."

A waiter came to enquire about dessert. Another waiter began clearing away the dinner dishes. He seemed curious about the fact that Ellie had left two-thirds of her food untouched but he said nothing. No one said anything until the waiters had departed, then she touched her lips with a napkin, put it back in her lap and picked up her own coffee cup.

"You're right, Morgan. I *have* put some other things together to form a pattern."

"Ellie, I want to extract one promise from you in exchange for what I've done for you."

"All right."

"I want your word you'll never tell your grandfather what you know."

She scowled. She specifically wanted to confront *him*. As far as Arthur Cartier was concerned, as Morgan had said, it made her sick, thinking back to his promises, to the way he'd played his part so perfectly, to the way he had used her, had used Jane Forrest and her father, to the way he'd used everyone. She felt only revulsion for Arthur, but towards her slyly intervening grandfather she felt indignation.

He seemed to understand, for after removing the pipe he said very earnestly, "I insist on that, and I won't settle for a compromise, Ellie. You will never tell the old man you know anything about what he has done. Never."

"Morgan, my grandfather deliberately, underhandedly in fact, meddled in my life. That's what originally caused all the trouble between my father and Grandfather Morris. And he still went ahead and meddled. I think it's despicable."

Morgan blew smoke at her, his eyes were toughly narrowed. "Damn it, I wish you'd grow up," he growled. "Sure he meddled; maybe he's done it all along, I don't know. I don't really care. But I'll tell you one thing, Ellie, that old man was right; he knew what kind of a fake Cartier was, and he knew as you *should* have known, if you'd had the sense God gave a goose, that if you'd married Cartier he'd have broken not just your heart but also your spirit. And the old man intervened. *That,* duck, is love. Not all this wishy-washy trash they put in motion pictures."

"It was wrong. He had no right!"

"He had every right," said Morgan, removing the pipe and fiercely gripping it. "The same as I have every right to demand your word of honour that you'll never breathe a word of what I've told you to him!"

"And if I refuse, Morgan?"

He sat still for a moment, then rose, picked her coat from the back of her chair and said, "Get up. I'm going to take you home!"

She obeyed. She'd never seen him genuinely angry before. It was slightly chilling. He was large and wide-shouldered, and now all that was magnified by the rocky set of his jaw and the unyielding deep fire in his glance.

He paid the cashier, puffed smoke like a locomotive and led her out into the warm and soft-bright night where they'd left his car. He held the door for her with an attitude of almost exaggerated courtesy, and as they were driving off and she said, "Morgan, we don't have to fight do we?" his answer came back sharply and coldly.

"Of course not. All you have to do is convince me you're more grown up than you've acted up to now, tonight."

That stung her anew. "Grown up! If I *weren't* grown up I could tolerate other people interfering in my life; I could act like a little girl and accept the tenet that Grandfather knows best."

"He *does*. In this instance he sure as hell does know best!"

"Don't you dare swear at me, Morgan Harding!"

He turned, "I didn't swear at you. I wouldn't swear at you even if I thought you needed it. Like a damned good paddling."

She balled up both fists and fought a valiant battle to control the boiling fury within. She had never before been truly angry with him, but she was now. So angry, in fact, that shortly before they pulled up out front of the house she said, "I hope I never see you again!"

He answered promptly. "You never will, believe me. Not if you go to your grandfather and throw one of these temper tantrums."

She squeezed both eyes tightly closed to help control the rage. It worked, but when she slowly opened them again they were halting out front of the house and that diverted her, too.

He climbed out, came round to her side, opened the door and stood stiffly, forbiddingly, glaring down as she climbed out and faced him.

She said, "Good-*night* — and — thank you for the dinner."

"It was lousy," he retorted. "Good-*night!*"

It didn't dawn upon her until, standing out front with the door key in her hand, that something he'd said just might have a frightful significance. He'd said, in response to her angry remark about never wanting to see him again, that she never would. Now, standing outside in the lovely night, she wondered if he'd meant that he would leave Windsor?

That made her heart sink still lower; if he left, how would it affect her father in his new business? She had the answer to that while still standing out there with the key in her hand, unwilling to open the door and walk in, because her parents were still sitting in the parlour and would most certainly want her to pause and tell them what a fine time she'd had on her date.

Finally, she went slowly round to the back door, entered that way without making any noise, got to her back bedroom without difficulty, and in the darkness went to stand by the window and gaze down at the empty kerbing where Morgan had halted to let her out.

She draped her coat upon a chair, kicked off her shoes, loosened her hair, her blouse, sank down on the side of the bed and tried to cry.

She couldn't.

CHAPTER SIXTEEN

"GOODBYE, ARTHUR"

She was up early the following morning, had breakfast prepared by the time her mother got to the kitchen, and in response to her mother's curiosity about the night before, simply said the dinner had been very good.

Alice knew the roadhouse. She could agree that the roast beef was exemplary. But what she was most curious about concerned Ellie's use of the back door when she'd got home.

"We didn't know you were in," she said. "Neither of us heard the car, and when we were ready for bed and I looked into your room, there you were, already asleep."

Alice watched her daughter from the stove and Ellie knew she was being watched. She tried to pass it off as of no importance.

George Jarrett came to the kitchen freshly scrubbed and shaved. He was usually in good spirits in the morning. He startled Ellie with an almost breezy remark.

"Had a quarrel last night, eh? Well, every couple I've ever known always has 'em."

He pecked his wife on the cheek, sat at the kitchen table and went to work on the breakfast Alice set before him.

Ellie, with no appetite, marvelled that he could eat so heartily, act so casual. But of course he did not know what Ellie knew. She was confident that if he *had* known he wouldn't have been able to eat either.

There was something else; she was still troubled by that statement of Morgan's about never seeing each other again. Not entirely for her own loss, but as it would reflect upon her father.

She wondered about telling him as he sat cheerily eating breakfast, but didn't quite have the courage for it.

Her father departed moments later, in a rush as usual, and as she helped her mother with the dishes, she debated again. Of course everyone was in some way involved. What her father had treated so cavalierly as a little lover's quarrel, would have stricken him dumb if he'd known what that disagreement had been about. Even Ellie's mother, usually on the fringe of things, and conciliatory by nature, would have been shocked to discover what her father had done.

It occurred to Ellie later, when she and her mother were giving the house a thorough cleaning, that quite possibly this might be part of the reason why Morgan wanted her never to mention what she knew.

Of course he'd heard, just like everyone else had, of that earlier unpleasantness at Grandfather Morris's mansion, and he could be relied upon to realise that this second case of patriarchal meddling, being more serious and direct, would cause an even greater breach. Could, very likely, cause a schism within the family that would never be healed.

She melted a little.

Then she asked herself a simple question: If she said nothing, what would prevent Grandfather Morris from meddling again, and again! She knew from snatches of things she'd heard around the house, that he made a habit of interfering in the lives of his family, and she also knew that, like her father, she would never tolerate anything like that. In fact, feeling much less of an obligation to the old man than her father had felt all those years, she would not stand for Grandfather Morris meddling in her life at all, now or later.

A car drew up outside and Alice came along to announce the arrival of Arthur Cartier. Ellie was in no mood for this confrontation although she'd had no illusions about eventually having to go through with it. She thanked her mother, pulled off the light scarf she'd wrapped round her hair, removed her house-cleaning apron and made a swift decision on strategy. She did not want her mother to hear what she had to say to Arthur, so she hastened forth and met him outside on the front porch.

He looked slightly stern, which she thought must be the role he'd chosen to enact this morning. It made her feel faint disgust. It also made her aware, finally, of what it was about Arthur that wore her down every time she was with him;

what it was that roiled her emotions, upset her balance and left her feeling exhausted.

He was always in command. His acting always dominated the scene even when he did not have to act at all. He used everyone as a foil, kept them defensively passive while he deflected his swiftly-changing moods off them.

Now, still with that faint expression of sternness, he greeted her, took her two hands and said, "It's all over. I gave old Forrest back the money and I told Janie there was no engagement. I kept my word to you, love, as you knew I'd do."

She freed her hands, turned and led him along the porch towards the sports car he'd left casually parked in the driveway. She debated which approach to use, selected her words carefully as she strolled along with Arthur beside her, and when they went down the steps off the porch she said, "Arthur, why did you do it?"

He stopped as though aghast. "Why? Ellie, what kind of a question is that? For love of you, of course. You know that."

She stepped into garage-shade although there was no real warmth yet, it was too early, and she looked him squarely in the eye, her expression soft and tender. "But I didn't think you loved me any more, Arthur."

"How *could* you think such a thing, Ellie."

Smiling sweetly, she then said, "I'm convinced, Arthur. Everything is as it was before, then. I'm so terribly relieved." She reached out to him as she said, "When do we leave?"

The shadow of sudden consternation that momentarily touched his brow then was gone, was what she'd wanted to see. She knew that part of Grandfather Morris's ultimatum had been for Arthur to leave Windsor *alone*. It required no powers of deduction worth mentioning to understand Grandfather Morris's basic reason in buying Arthur off had been to prevent his granddaughter from being taken away.

Arthur didn't falter, he was too good an actor for that, but his next words confirmed what she already suspected. "Ellie, I've got to go alone. I mean, there's just so much that must be done in New York. You understand. It's not that I don't *want* to take you, believe me, it's simply that. . . ." Arthur rolled his eyes and made a little weak gesture of resignation with his hands. "Work and more work, love. Day and night. And although you'd be an inspiration, it wouldn't be fair to you."

She couldn't listen to any more. Dropping her arms, she stepped back to lean upon the front wall of the garage and study him coldly as she said, "Stop it! Arthur, you're a very dangerous liar. Most people have trouble with a conscience when they lie. Not you. If you were smarter, more gifted, more intelligent and not such a total egotist, you'd be a very dangerous man. You're the kind of person who could propagandise ignorant and uninformed people, making them militants."

He stood gazing at her, and probably it wasn't her words nor their meaning that held him speechless as much as it was the expression of utter revulsion on her face. He didn't even offer to interrupt, which was unusual, because normally, in order to hold the initiative, he over-rode what others had to say.

"Arthur, my grandfather paid you to go away without me. He bought you body and soul. That's why you gave Mister Forrest back the fifty thousand dollars and why you broke your engagement to Janie. You did those things ruthlessly, the same as you stood in my parlour the night before last and played the part of an outraged and wronged lover."

Ellie paused, seeking fresh words. The revulsion she showed so plainly made it difficult to be perfectly rational. She took so long preparing the ensuing sentences he finally spoke.

"You don't know what you're talking about. No one buys Arthur Cartier!"

She spat a word at him she borrowed from Morgan Harding. "You phony, Arthur. You despicable fake. Breaking Janie's heart meant no more to you than ditching me because you knew, after my father's quarrel with my grandfather, I would be no source of money to you.

"You cultivated Janie to get fifty thousand dollars from her father. My grandfather knew you that well without ever having sat down and talked to you. It goes against the grain to tell you this, Arthur, but my grandfather was right about you all along — and I was wrong.

"*He* knew he was right. He proved it. You agreed to do whatever he said for one hundred and fifty thousand dollars!"

Arthur lit a cigarette with a little flourish and assumed a worldly, blasé stance and said, "Ellie, I didn't recognise it before, but you'd make a great emotional actress. I almost wish I'd seen you really upset before the old man and I had our little talk. I might have turned him down in order to manage you on the stage."

"Talk," she said flatly, "more lies, more self-delusion. I hope you never have to wake up, Arthur, and see yourself as you really are."

"You believed in me, love. Remember that."

"And I'm degraded because of it. I'm ashamed that I was such a small-town innocent."

He exhaled smoke at her, his beautiful violet eyes as steady as stone without a hint of remorse or shame or even embarrassment because she'd stripped him naked of all shame. Then he flipped his shoulders in a slight, callous little shrug and said, "Okay, Ellie, okay. But there's one thing you've overlooked: I didn't have to come to you the other night. I didn't have to come here this morning. But I did it. Can you give me an answer to that?"

"Because your ego wouldn't let you leave me without playing one last tragic role."

"No," he softly said, holding her eyes with his violet stare. "Because you really meant something to me. Look, assuming you're right — and I'm not admitting it, mind — but assuming it's all as you've said it is — my logical course was to pack up, load the car and leave Windsor yesterday, or this morning. Instead, here I am, seeing you for the last time — because I've known your love and have returned it with my own." He dropped the half-smoked cigarette, stamped it out, raised his face and smiled a little sadly. "It *was* love, on both sides, Ellie, whether you want to believe that now or not."

She felt the confusion rising up from within as she'd felt it before when he'd told her things she was not conditioned by environment to accept nor believe. She sought for words and found none, and Arthur, watching her closely, knew exactly what her trouble was, had always been able to divine her secret turmoils. He was about to speak again, when she heard herself speaking.

"You never really loved me, Arthur. You loved yourself. I was the reflection of that. You saw yourself through my eyes; you fed on my adoration of you. Arthur, I feel sad for you: *You are incapable of giving love to anyone.*"

As she uttered those last eight words their true meaning sank searingly into her consciousness with a peculiar effect. She stood staring at him, seeing for the first time that, perhaps in order for his acting ability to be so pre-eminent, something much more human and worthwhile and desirable had been entirely omitted from his character. He was a genuine misfit, a genuine psychopathic misfit. Possibly that was what her grandfather had meant, although he hadn't expressed it that way, when he'd said actors were not stable people.

He leaned, missing his cue entirely, for instead of acting the role of a saddened, pathetic man, he smiled and said, "One last kiss, pet, then we sink into one another's memories never to touch again in this life."

It made her feel a little ill, the way Morgan had predicted. She had no idea what play those words were from and she didn't care, But she knew as well as she knew her own name they were not original; knew that behind them was absolutely no meaning for him at all.

"Janie needs the kiss, Arthur, not I." She moved a little to avoid personal contact with him.

He drew erect and wagged his head very slightly. "Janie needs the same thing you do, pet; she needs a nice five-day-a-week husband with a nice little stuffy office, a nice little hypocritical job in a nice little downtown building, so that some day she — and you — can raise more nice little stuffy middle-class children, while the true geniuses of this stinking world can go on creating beauty and art and truth, unburdened by middle-class virtues — and wives."

She listened and shook her head, and finally said, "Good-bye, Arthur."

He didn't answer although he had ample time to do so as he strolled around to the far side of his car, got in, revved up the motor and without a wave or even a final glance, engaged gears, backed clear, and went driving away through a gorgeous morning.

CHAPTER SEVENTEEN

IT ISN'T ENDED

Alice's brother Carleton dropped by later, and although Ellie heard his car in the driveway and saw him alight, she was bathing and had no opportunity to go into the parlour — nor, for the matter of that, much inclination either — so she leisurely bathed and afterwards got dressed in the same way, by which time she was sure her uncle had departed, and finally, with the sun beginning to turn faintly red as it dropped down the sky a bit, she went out into the front of the house.

She was correct, Uncle Carleton had gone. Her mother was sewing in a wing-chair beside the front window and swung a little to look out as Ellie came forward.

Alice said, "Uncle Carleton was here," as though she understood her daughter's reluctance to come forth while her brother had been present. "He rather wanted to see you, I think."

"Whatever for?"

"There's been some trouble," replied Alice in a low, slow-paced tone.

Ellie sank down close by, watching as her mother resumed sewing, each movement calm and deliberate. Like gardening, Alice was addicted to periods of needlework, usually when the weather outside was too foul to permit gardening. She didn't raise her head as she said, "Jane Forrest tried to do away with herself this morning; they pumped her stomach at the hospital."

Ellie was as still as stone. Her mother looked up, grave and thoughtful, then lowered her head and considered the work she'd been doing as she spoke on.

"But that's not what would bring your uncle out. He only mentioned that because he thought it might interest us. What really brought him was something he considers much more critical. It seems Grandfather Morris has squandered a fortune, and Carleton, when he discovered it, was so aghast that he wants the family to meet at his house tomorrow night to consider having Grandfather Morris declared incompetent."

Ellie had to consider that a moment before commenting. The reason she had to consider was elemental; she thought she knew what fortune her uncle had found out that Grandfather Morris had squandered.

"I'll go visit Janie this evening," she said, clearing that out of the way. "Mother, did Uncle Carleton tell you about the money Grandfather squandered?"

"Only the amount, Ellie, which was a hundred and fifty thousand dollars, and to whom he gave it."

Ellie watched her mother's face. Alice was concentrating on the sewing and did not look at her daughter as they spoke. Ellie deduced, from this attitude of avoidance, that her mother either knew or suspected what had happened. She took down a big breath and said, "Mother, Grandfather gave that money to Arthur Cartier to buy him off. In exchange Arthur is to leave Windsor, probably never to return, and he is not to take anyone, primarily me I suppose, with him. Grandfather Morris is still ruling our lives."

Alice raised calm eyes and gently, rather absently, smiled. "Is that a fact?"

Ellie had a sudden twinge. She could imagine the look of condemnation on Morgan Harding's face when he discovered Ellie had given away their secret. She also had an uneasy feeling that none of what she'd just said had really shocked her mother at all. Of course, with Alice, it was sometimes a little hard to tell; she was actually placid by nature. Even when surprised or agitated, she did not react with any sudden outbursts.

Alice, satisfied with her mending job, put the sewing articles in their little basket, looked at Ellie and said, "Carleton did not know *why* that money had been spent as Grandfather Morris spent it, but he knew to whom it had been given, and his reaction was normal, I think. He said there was no excuse under the sun for your grandfather, at his age, to buy into some high-risk Broadway stage production; that Grandfather Morris had to be losing his judgement to do such a thing, and in order to protect the business as well as the family from anything as foolish in the future, steps must be taken."

Alice smiled and her eyes twinkled. Ellie was unsure what this presaged, but her mother did not keep her in suspense very long.

"I told him that according to the by-laws of the family corporation as I'd had them explained to me by my husband, father was paid an annual salary, and that otherwise he had only *emeritus* status with Morris and Morris." Alice's twinkle became more pronounced. "That's actually your father's word. But I used it anyway; sounds so knowledgeable, don't you think? I told him that if he and Michael chose to bow to father every time he barked at them, that was their affair, but that I not only wouldn't attend any meeting designed to hurt father, I would even take father's side against them, and I'd see that your father hired John Forrest to help."

Ellie felt a little exasperated. She'd got rid of one problem and here was the threat of an even greater problem; trouble within the family, with her, basically, as the cause. She said, "What was Uncle Carleton's reaction?"

"He was indignant with me."

"Mother, he doesn't know why Grandfather gave Arthur that money. If he knew. . . ." Ellie let it trail off as she and her mother exchanged a long look.

"You'd be wasting your breath, child," said Alice. "I've known your uncle a lot longer than you have. Nothing that stems from the heart, the emotions, would be a cash commodity in his sight. He's a business man and nothing else."

"Will he and Michael go ahead and try to have Grandfather declared incompetent?"

Alice didn't know, but she had one pertinent comment to make on that possibility. "If they think father has been cantankerous upon other occasions, child, if they've flinched when he roared at them, believe me, Carleton and Michael would simply disintegrate when Grandfather Morris discovers what they have in mind, *this* time."

Be that as it may, in Ellie's view the issue went far beyond an old man's cry of outrage. She understood what her mother had said about the reason Grandfather Morris had spent that money being unintelligible and unacceptable to her uncle, but she also knew that the notoriety sure to ensure if this battle was joined between father and son would be terribly humiliating to them all.

She rose and went to stand by a front window, fists clenched, wishing with all her heart and soul that she had never set eyes on Arthur Cartier. But that mood of frustrated exasperation only lasted a moment; it was, after all, not a very sensible wish at this late date.

She turned to find her mother eyeing her. "Arthur is gone. I told him a few minutes ago that he was a liar, a fake, and incapable of genuine deep feelings for anyone."

Alice was gentle with her rejoinder to all that.

"Quite a speech, child. Are you sure he's gone?"

"I'm sure that was part of his deal with Grandfather, and Arthur won't welsh on a hundred and fifty thousand dollars, Mother, although he might welsh on something as archaic and middle-class as his word of honour."

"Fine," said Alice briskly, rising and taking the sewing basket with her. "Then it seems to me what we need now is our own council of war. You, your father, me. . . ." Alice started towards the kitchen. ". . . and of course Morgan Harding. Would you like a chicken sandwich, Ellie? I thought I'd make one."

Alice was through the dining-room midway to the kitchen door before Ellie turned. It was too late for an immediate retort on including Morgan Harding in their family conference. Alice disappeared beyond the kitchen door.

Ellie turned to resume her earlier study of the garden out front where molten sunshine like new gold lay everywhere.

She was honest with herself.

Morgan *did* have a part in what was happening. He'd had a part in what was past as well. In fact, the more she thought about it, the more it appeared that Morgan *was* a part of everything that had been shaping and forming her life lately.

Her mother, speaking from the kitchen doorway, said, "Child, if you're going to visit Janie at the hospital you'd better start getting ready. Visiting hours are from two in the afternoon until four. And I've left a chicken sandwich on the kitchen table for you. Now I've got to go do some shopping."

A few moments later, when her mother's car coughed to life out in the garage, Ellie took the plate with the sandwich on it to a window and watched her mother drive away. Then she went to the table, sat and finished the sandwich. It was exceptionally good, or she was exceptionally hungry, but in either event the entire sandwich disappeared.

Later, while dressing for the hospital visit, she recalled most of what Morgan had told her that night they'd got so angry at one another, but instead of becoming indignant all over again, she picked out the kernels of truth and mulled them over.

It was never pleasant, of course, admitting error. It was particularly odious when one had been told so bluntly and emphatically that one was wrong, and to top it all off, having taken comfort from the knowledge that her father had been righteously outraged over Grandfather Morris's meddling, it was now very evident that Grandfather Morris wasn't just right, but he'd also been making substantial sacrifices for the family, in this instance, for Ellie herself.

On the way to the hospital, which sat upon a little landscaped knoll east of town where it was usually visible from all directions, she made a calm decision to go see Morgan at his office when she finished her visit with Janie Forrest.

She even smiled a little over having to eat crow;

if that unpalatable dish had to be eaten, then it would be nice to have to do so with him.

She didn't speculate on why this should be because the entrance to the hospital parking area loomed up, and after passing through it she was occupied with the need for locating a parking space. Evidently everyone who had an ailing friend or relative was visiting them today.

Inside, she was directed to Janie's room, and, expecting to find others there, she was relieved to find only an enormous bank of flowers, and the ill girl, whose dark, sultry beauty seemed very appealing against the white of her bedclothes.

They were a little awkward to one another at first, until Ellie drew up a chair and said, "There are a lot of damn fools in this world, aren't there, Jane?"

The dark girl's eyes slowly kindled with ironic understanding. "The hell of it is, Ellie, they are all female."

The ice was broken. Ellie admired the flowers and Jane Forrest said, "It's like a hothouse in here — or an undertaking parlour."

Ellie smiled, considered the ill girl's pallor, her troubled eyes, and said, "Odd how labels come off bottles. I almost did the same thing you did one time — got the wrong bottle."

Janie shook her head. "No one would believe it now, Ellie. I don't really care very much anyway. I loved him. I'll admit it. I'm beginning to think my father is right. He says the best thing that ever happened, for my sake, was to have

Arthur turn out to be such an unmitigated heel — *before* I got any more involved."

Ellie patted Jane's hand. "It's over anyway. He's gone."

"Is he? Did you talk to him?"

"This morning. It wasn't a very pleasant parting. He's gone, and I suppose that's the most important thing."

"There's a rumour going round, Ellie, that someone loaned him a fortune to go down to New York and produce a play. My father told me that, when he was in a little while ago. I wonder if it's really true."

Ellie smiled and rose, confident Jane Forrest's near-fatal depression was not likely to recur. She didn't mention what she was thinking: That if Jane's father had heard that rumour, being as shrewd and knowledgeable as he was, he would also either know definitely or have a very good idea who had bought Arthur off.

"I'll be back," she said.

"No need," replied the girl in the bed. "I'm going home in the morning. By the way, did you ever have your stomach pumped?"

"No. Pretty bad?"

"There's not a man on earth who's worth going through that for, Ellie."

They laughed together and Ellie went to the door, turned and said, "I'll come by the house. Okay?"

"I'd like that very much. Promise you will?"

"I promise."

Back outside in the growing lateness of afternoon Ellie felt very calm, very mature, as she got into the car and drove back down towards the centre of town for the next errand she had to run.

CHAPTER EIGHTEEN

DIFFERENT ATTITUDES

Morgan, a receptionist in her father's front office told Ellie, was over at the Morris & Morris warehouse. He would probably be back shortly, if Miss Jarrett would care to wait, although it was just as possible that he would keep right on working past quitting time because he frequently did so.

Ellie's private feelings were of relief, but she also faced the fact that putting off apologising to Morgan only made it harder. She left no message, thanked the girl and left the building. It didn't occur to her right then that the girl would either tell Morgan personally or leave him a note, saying who his caller had been.

She was beside the car ready to climb in when her uncle appeared across the street, waved and hastened over. She waited politely, but wished mightily there'd been some way to avoid doing so, wished she might have seen Carleton first so that she could have pretended that she hadn't.

He was jovial, which was not his usual manner, as he came up and said, "Missed you at the house today, Heloise. I was sorry about that, but I suppose your mother told you the purpose of my visit."

She nodded, studying him and wondering how

much, if anything at all, he had learned since he'd called by the house. "We'd been house cleaning," she said, being cautious. "It takes a long while to clean up afterwards."

He brushed that aside, driving directly towards the point of his earlier visit, which was obviously also his reason for buttonholing her now. "I was sorry your mother took the attitude she took, Heloise, towards my proposal of a family meeting. I'm sure you're as much aware as the rest of us must be, that Grandfather Morris simply can't be allowed to bankrupt himself on such foolish things as stage plays."

"Uncle Carleton, how much money is Grandfather Morris worth?"

Carleton could guess at once what his answer was going to do — give his niece ammunition for rebuttal. He cleared his throat and slid his glance away then back again before speaking.

Ellie didn't wait. "A hundred and fifty thousand dollars *is* a fortune, Uncle Carleton, but I'm under the impression Grandfather Morris is worth several millions."

"But that's exactly the point, child. We should be forewarned from this example of profligacy. Next time he may give away half a million or more."

Ellie stood gazing at the older man; she liked him but not as she liked other older men because he did not have the same warmth. Her mother's syllepsis had been accurate — Uncle Carleton was strictly a businessman, with every virtue and every vice that designation implied.

But where she was hung up now, was in trying to fathom Uncle Carleton's motives sufficiently to satisfy herself that they were founded upon genuine concern, or whether they were founded upon something else far less attractive.

He withstood her stare for a long moment, then said, "All right, Ellie, you do whatever you feel is proper. I won't try to influence you. Goodbye." He turned, went round the car, stepped on to the sidewalk and went briskly along in the direction he'd been walking when he'd seen her.

She decided his motives *were* genuine concern, not something else, got into the car and drove through late-day gloaming towards home. Her biggest surprise occurred when she entered the house and heard her grandfather's voice in the parlour. There was no car out front, no advance warning at all, but he didn't drive any more so perhaps she shouldn't have been too surprised.

Having entered through the back door she encountered her mother in the kitchen, and raised her brows quizzically. Alice said her father was in the parlour with Grandfather Morris, that they were discussing the inventory-audit system which Grandfather Morris had agreed to install, although he felt impelled to haggle loudly and somewhat profanely over the cost of it.

Alice winked. "Your grandfather was a horse-trader as a very young man. He could never abide people who paid the asking price without at least lamenting the debasement of our currency, the spiralling costs of organised labour, and the ruination brought upon the nation by the villainous Democratic party." Alice's smile lingered. "How is Janie?"

"She's going home in the morning," exclaimed Ellie, shedding her coat and gloves. "Mother, does Dad know Uncle Carleton was here today?"

"Yes. I had a chance to tell him before your grandfather arrived."

"Did you tell him *why* Grandfather gave Arthur the money?"

Alice nodded. "I told why we *thought* Arthur got the money. But actually, child, we don't *know*, do we?"

Ellie knew. She thought her mother should also be convinced, but on the other hand her mother wasn't as immersed in the entire affair as Ellie was, so perhaps it was possible for her to have reservations. Alice wouldn't *like* to believe the real reason, therefore she wouldn't want to believe it. Without iron-clad proof she'd drift along as she was now doing. That was her nature.

Alice said, "Your father agrees with me about Uncle Carleton's suggestion. He said it was barbarous and inhuman."

Ellie sank down at the kitchen table and said, "Mother, this is the damnedest family I've ever known."

"Heloise Jarrett; what kind of language that!"

Ellie smiled, for although Alice had just heard her own family impugned, she was only upset over one negligible word of casual profanity.

"Last month, Mother, Father was ready to carve the hearts out of everyone named Morris. Now, he's sitting in there with Grandfather, firmly prepared to defend an old man's prerogatives."

"Well," exclaimed Alice, "I don't see anything so frightful about that. After all, a lot of things happened last month that look quite different *this* month. *Last* month you were being just barely civil to Morgan Harding and couldn't get through the day unless you either saw Arthur Cartier or spoke to him on the telephone."

Ellie said, "*Touché*, Mother."

Alice bit her lip in quick confusion. "I'm sorry, sweetheart. It just popped into mind and I said it. There are much better examples." She grinned weakly. "Only when I get a little annoyed I can never think straight. Now you'd better go and get dressed for supper, child."

Ellie, neglecting to enter the parlour where those masculine voices rose and fell, did not do this for any reason other than that she was sure, whatever her father and grandfather were discussing, would be better off for not being interrupted.

But she was also beginning to feel tired, for, from the beginning of this day, and her disagreement with Arthur, up until just now when she'd learnt her grandfather was at the house, a lot had been drained out of her.

What she'd have *liked* to have done would have been take a hot bath and perhaps watch television for an hour or so, then go to bed.

Alice came to the bedroom door as she was stepping out of the street dress she'd worn to the hospital to say Morgan Harding had just called to say he'd drop by this evening.

Then her mother stood in the doorway brightly looking straight at Ellie. "Well, child . . . ?"

"Well, what, Mother? If he's coming by I won't have enough time to dig a moat or erect a Berlin Wall, will I?"

Alice stiffened. "If you were ten years younger I'd take the hairbrush to you!"

Ellie smiled. "I'm bushed, Mother. Worn down to a frazzle. I apologise."

Alice hesitated, turning solicitous. "I'd call him and suggest perhaps tomorrow might be better, except that I haven't the faintest idea where to reach him. Well, hurry and get ready for dinner, child, it won't be long."

After her mother had gone Ellie stood silently laughing at her own reflection in the mirror. There were two telephone directories, one near the telephone stand in the front hallway, another in the kitchen. Morgan Harding would be listed in both. But even if he were not listed, all one had ever had to do in Windsor to reach a person whose number one did not have, was to ask the switchboard girl; she would always oblige.

But having a transparent mother, Ellie mused, was probably better than having a devious and brooding one. It had started with Grandfather Morris. At least he had been violently opposed to Arthur. Then Morgan had come along. It had never been any secret, actually, that both Ellie's parents favoured her union with Morgan. It was no secret right this minute that the reason her mother had professed an inability to reach Morgan tonight was because she was as pleased as punch that he was coming by, after the quarrel.

Her father, when her mother had a chance to whisper the tidings to him, would also be as pleased as punch. It was even possible Grandfather Morris, who had once raised his cane threateningly against Morgan, but who had subsequently authorised his inventory-audit survey, might also take a benign view of this union.

She was at a loss to think of anyone who would *not* be favourable. Unless, of course, it was she, herself, and that was why she'd laughed at herself in the mirror. Everyone who denounced meddling, was happily, even actively, doing just exactly that.

She dressed carefully, continued to feel whimsical right up until she left her room and went out to the parlour to kiss her father's cheek, and to lean to also do the same to her grandfather, then she said, gazing with wide-eyed innocence at them, that Morgan Harding was coming by and she couldn't imagine why, since she'd told him she never wanted to see him again unless, of course, it had something to do with the inventory-audit system, in which case, that being strictly business, she'd excuse herself and help in the kitchen.

She could tell by the sudden still and discomfited look in both their eyes that their entire conversation in the parlour had *not* dealt exclusively with the inventory-audit system.

Her father tried being blustery. "Well now, Ellie, I hardly think you can adopt any such attitude towards young Harding right here in our house. After all, the laws of hospitality are —"

"Whoa," broke in Grandfather Morris, his face as coldly impersonal as it usually was when he had a pronouncement to make. "Just a moment, young lady. Let's not delude ourselves; you're nigh twenty. Your great-grandmother Heloise was married at sixteen; in her first child-bed by eighteen. Your own grandmother was married at seventeen. Your Uncle Carleton was born when she was exactly as old as you are right this minute. Now I think, Heloise, when a woman starts getting along a bit, she'd be wise not to be too careless about disposing of beaux."

Ellie wanted to laugh at them. The tiredness that had assailed her an hour earlier was mitigated by their transparent raffishness. Last month, at each other's throats over her, this month conniving secretly together to influence her life.

"Grandfather," she said, leaning to put a cool palm against his cheek and to smile directly and deeply into his eyes. "Do you know what I think?"

"Well. . . ."

Her father, suddenly afraid, cleared his throat in a threatening manner.

She continued to smile into the old man's pale,

faded eyes. "I think you're wonderful. Very wise, very generous, a lot more sagacious than anyone else in this crazy damned family."

The old man recoiled from that one word exactly as her mother had done, except that he also blushed. He hung there, at a loss. He certainly couldn't scold someone who'd just paid him the highest of compliments. Gradually, his eyes narrowed.

"Heloise, I think you're a vixen. By the Lord Harry's ghost I never thought that before, but all of a sudden I'm really seeing you as a grown woman."

Alice came to the dinning-room door to call them all to supper. There was no mention of an invitation to Grandfather Morris. There never was; when he arrived at someone's house at supper-time it was automatically assumed he was included, and he invariably accepted this as part of the homage due him.

Ellie helped him up, held his arm and as she went along with him, behind her uneasy father, She said, "No one is really worth that much money, Grandfather."

He looked up quickly, saw the steady way she was regarding him, sucked on his lips a moment then answered. "You're wrong, Heloise. Wrong as — hell. Wait until you're my age and you'll make a very devastating discovery. Money ain't worth a damn for anything at all except buying happiness with. Don't argue. Just wait until you're my age, *then* decide who is right, you or me."

CHAPTER NINETEEN

AN EVENING AT HOME

Grandfather Morris knew of his son's anxiety over the way he'd spent a hundred and fifty thousand dollars. Ellie never did discover *how* he knew, although she always suspected that her mother might have forewarned him.

His initial remark at the dinner table indicated he'd given this subject some thought. "You know, to have someone declared incompetent just isn't all that easy. Carleton may have my best interests at heart, but where is he going to find the witnesses an incompetency hearing requires?"

Grandfather Morris did not seem especially outraged, which was what Ellie had expected. In fact, he was quietly, almost casually, clinical in his approach, at least his *outward* approach, to the subject.

Ellie's thoughts during this discussion were direct. She was not concerned with the validity of the allegation, she was instead conscious of Grandfather Morris's clear and rational conversation. If he was incompetent, then she could think of dozens of people who were even more incompetent.

Alice maintained a demure but attentive attitude during the discussion of her father's alleged incompetence. She never once advanced an opinion although everyone at the supper table knew her adequately to appreciate that she *had* one.

But Grandfather Morris, with an devious lack of interest in Carleton's scheme, steered the conversation back to what was generally and commonly being called the Jarrett System now, meaning, of course, Morgan Harding's inventory-audit undertaking. This interested the old man above almost everything else, or at least he certainly laboured hard to give that impression.

He did not once mention Arthur Cartier. As a matter of fact, when Ellie reflected upon this, she could not recall ever having heard him mention Arthur in her presence, although she knew perfectly well he'd mentioned him before others, including her parents.

Listening to the old man now, watching him, Ellie was tempted to smile. He was an old iceberg — the one-third above water was far less impressive than the two thirds beneath the water.

The old man ate very little although he somehow managed to give the impression, perhaps because he was always the last one to rise from the table, of being a moderately heavy eater.

They were back in the parlour, Ellie's father and grandfather, and she was helping her mother clear away the dishes, when Ellie observed just how little Grandfather Morris actually did eat.

Alice explained about the lowered requirements of elderly, sedentary people, and during the course of this casual conversation, Morgan Harding arrived.

Ellie and her mother heard the door-chime, naturally, but it was Ellie's father who went to admit Morgan. When Ellie returned to the dining-room for the last of the dishes she saw him sitting in the parlour with her father and grandfather. Back in the kitchen, she said, "Return of the prodigal. Morgan's arrived. They are now giving him the third-degree in the parlour."

Alice looked up. "If you like, I'll rescue him."

Ellie picked up a clean dish-towel, shook her head. "It's a little awkward," she confessed, "having him here. I didn't invite him, but I suppose when he heard I'd been asking for him at the office this afternoon he thought . . . Well, he probably thought I'd come crawling to apologise."

Alice kept watching her daughter. "Not crawling, I'd risk a guess, child, but willing to apologise." She smiled. "To borrow a phrase of your father's — the hell of it is — someone always has to be the first to yield."

They laughed and went to work on the sinkful of dishes, and eventually Ellie detected the pleasant aroma of a pipe. Her mother was curious, since neither Ellie's father nor grandfather used pipes, until Ellie explained, then she said she'd always loved the fragrance of good tobacco.

Ellie's retort was basic. "I don't know good tobacco from bad. But his pipe *does* smell good, doesn't it?"

"How about good *men?*" asked Alice softly,

and became quite occupied with scouring the inside of a pan when Ellie turned a wide-eyed look in her direction.

Ellie did not reply to that and Alice was content to let it pass. It evidently had been one of those spur-of-the-moment remarks anyway.

Moments later their attention was attracted by the sound of a car starting out in the driveway. Alice went to a window to peer out. "Mister Harding's car," she said, returning to the sink. "Isn't he leaving rather soon after arriving?"

Ellie was nonplussed. She'd had some idea he'd come by to see her. But at the same window she saw his car backing away. It had been parked directly behind her father's car.

She turned back to drying dishes with a let-down feeling, but she said nothing. Of course she didn't have to, after all, Alice had studied her daughter's moods for almost twenty years, she knew the one into which Ellie had fallen now, and she tried as she always had in the past, to break the spell.

She said, "It is getting on towards ten o'clock. I'm sure he's had a long, hard day. You need your beauty-rest, too, Ellie. Anyway, he'll be back."

There just weren't too many variables Alice could put into her mitigating effort but she made a valiant effort.

"Suppose we have another little supper tomorrow night and ask your father to bring Mister Harding home with him? It seems to me this

Jarrett System is absorbing too much of everyone's time, and that includes your father's time. He doesn't talk about very much else these days."

Ellie rallied enough to shake her head. She didn't actually veto her mother's suggestion but she scuttled it by suggesting that perhaps, until the Jarrett System was functioning smoothly, it might not be too successful, trying to get the men involved in the social amenities. She then said she'd go get the ashtrays from the parlour to be emptied and washed, and went out of the kitchen, through the dining-room and into the parlour.

She no more expected to meet the composed gaze of Morgan Harding in the otherwise empty parlour than she'd have expected to find Arthur Cartier sitting there relaxed, smoking a pipe.

Morgan put the pipe aside, uncrossed his long legs and rose with a soft little amiable smile into her surprised eyes. "Your father took your grandfather home," he explained, then, seeing that the surprise did not atrophy, he explained further. "I parked my car directly behind you father's car, which was stupid of me. Your father used my car. He couldn't get his car out without moving mine, anyway."

Ellie said, "Oh. Well, it just startled me, finding you still here."

Morgan considered her a moment, then said, "I can leave, Ellie. I guess I should have volunteered to take your grandfather home. The thought occurred to me, but I didn't mention it because I thought you might be around." He paused, his expression turned slightly saturnine, then he added: "But if you'd prefer, I'll wait outside."

That annoyed her. "Don't be ridiculous. Sit down, please."

He sat, resumed his smiling expression and ran a roving eye over her. "You look very pretty tonight. You usually do, though."

That amused her, for some reason. Not many men said a woman *usually* looked pretty, implying that they did not *always* appear attractive. She was self-conscious, standing there rather like a stranger in her own parlour, and as the little silence between them ran on, she groped about for the words she'd rehearsed earlier, and couldn't find a single one of them.

"Well," she said finally, "I dropped by the office this afternoon. . . ."

"So our receptionist said. That's why I came round tonight. To apologise for my terrible manners last night. The only excuse I can offer, Ellie, is that I've been under a lot of strain this past week or two. Of course, there's no reason for taking it out on you."

She went forward to a chair, sat and smiled at him. "It was really my fault, Morgan. I inherited some of my father's temper. I usually try to control it, but sometimes not very successfully, I'm afraid. That's what I wanted to tell you today, on my way back from the hospital."

He shrewdly and gently eased the topic to

something else; they had both confessed to being contrite, there could be no point in belabouring the point. "You saw Jane Forrest?"

She nodded. "Just for a few minutes. She'll be going home in the morning."

"It wasn't too serious then, I take it."

"They pumped her stomach in time, I guess." Recalling Jane's appraisal of that uncomfortable procedure made Ellie smile. But she didn't say that Jane's experience had left her convinced no man was worth going through such an ordeal. She simply said, "She'll recover in every way that counts — in a short time."

He nodded, leaned to ream his pipe into an ashtray and pocket it as he said, "How about you, Ellie? Will you recover in a short while, too?"

"You mean about — Arthur?"

He nodded, settling back again in the chair, his eyes fully on her. "Yes, about Cartier."

This, of course, was her real confession to him. She was aware of that even as she nodded her head. "He came by this morning. It seems a lifetime ago. But it wasn't very difficult for me, Morgan. Unlike Janie, I had tons of hard-headed advice."

She smiled and he smiled back. She wasn't actually being sarcastic but the implication was amply clear, what she'd meant was that everyone, Morgan included, had told her by word or action that Arthur just wasn't for her.

With a little wagging finger in the attitude of a parent admonishing a child, but in this instance teasingly, he said, "Always listen to your elders, duck."

"I always have, although I can't say their overwhelming wisdom has invariably been infallible."

She relaxed. He had a way about him that she'd only seen in one other man — her father — that could slide gracefully past awkward moments making things whimsically right again. All that wrath and venom of the other night was erased. She supposed that *he* would never forget it, and she was positive *she* never would, but at least his attitude now seemed to say it was past, part of their growing and continuing awareness of one another; that it was a hard lesson both had learned, something they should both profit from, but otherwise not to be recalled.

It was pleasant being alone in the parlour with him now. It was also a relief when he smiled and laughed, and teased her. All the day-long tension aggravated by the knowledge that she would apologise when they met, was magically gone.

"Had a little irrelevancy to tell your father tonight," he said, apropos of nothing they'd discussed thus far. "Ran into Michael Morris on my way home from the office. To fully confess, I was done-in, worn-out, in the vernacular, duck, I was beat. There's a little bar a block or two from the Larimore Building. I stopped there for a pick-me-up."

She was surprised. "Michael was in a *bar?*"

"Don't look so aghast. Michael's got red corpuscles just like everyone else. Yeah, he was in there hoisting a couple before heading home. I guess he'd had a hard day, too. I'd have retreated if I'd seen him in time; the last thing I wanted was to renew our altercation in a public bar. But he wasn't sloshed, and when I climbed on to the stool and ordered, there he was right beside me nursing a martini. I think he was even more surprised than I was."

"What happened, Morgan?"

"He bought my drink, I stood the next round, then we decided we'd both quit."

"Is that all?"

"Not quite. He said I sure could hit hard. He also said Carleton and Grandfather Morris and your father were perfectly right; that he'd been a heel. It was a little embarrassing. Then he offered his hand and we shook. He said the Jarrett System was to be installed and he was glad of that, that he approved of it one hundred per cent. Then we went outside together and he said something I didn't quite understand; something about Carleton making a fool of himself over a hundred and fifty thousand dollars."

Ellie rose. "Wouldn't you like a cup of coffee, Morgan?"

He considered a moment then also rose. "I'd love one."

She smiled as they came close. "You know what he meant about that money, Morgan."

"No, not entirely, love. Of course the *amount* rang a bell."

"Come out in the kitchen and I'll explain while

I'm fixing the coffee."

For a second he teetered there and she thought he was going to take her in his arms, then the swift little unnerving moment passed and he said, "Lead the way, lovely lady."

CHAPTER TWENTY

AN END TO MEMORY

Morgan was shocked at Carleton Morris's attitude towards the way Grandfather Morris was spending his money. He was inclined to agree that buying Arthur Cartier off for a hundred and fifty thousand dollars was highway robbery, but, as he said, that was no longer the issue.

Alice, having discreetly excused herself shortly after welcoming Morgan to the spotless kitchen, was no longer around. Except for Morgan and Ellie the kitchen was empty.

She allowed his coffee to percolate exactly ten minutes — her father's avowed recipe — and had one cup with him. He was on his second cup when he said he couldn't understand Carleton's attitude.

His reasons were basically similar to the ones Ellie also believed in. "It's the old man's money. If he wants to spend it on a rat — or if he wants to use it for endowing a Himalayan rest-house — darned if I see that it's anyone's business but his own."

Ellie concurred quietly. "I think that's the general attitude in the family. Uncle Carleton told me today, out front of your building incidentally, that he wasn't altogether concerned about the hundred and fifty thousand; he was worried for fear Grandfather Morris might spend an even greater amount on something else equally as — foolish."

Morgan put the coffee cup aside, made a wry face and said, "If that old man is incompetent I'm a monkey's uncle. I've argued with him, I've discussed details and procedures with him, and I've been interrogated by him. His mind's as sharp as a tack. Incompetent my foot!"

"You're getting carried away, Morgan. You're getting loud."

He grinned. "You know what I think? Aside from you, your father and your mother, the Morrisses are a rare nest of birds."

"Careful now," Ellie admonished. "I'm honour-bound to spring to the defence of the clan."

Morgan sat a moment in quiet thought before he spoke again. "Ellie, you know your uncle much better than I do. Would he actually go through with something like this? I mean, would he subject the entire family to a courtroom brawl, with the newspapers carrying the account blow by blow?"

She had asked herself that question several times. Part of the time she didn't believe her uncle had the nerve to go through with it. Part of the time she was almost convinced that he *would* do it. She could not give him the unqualified answer he sought, and a moment later, when he asked her grandfather's reaction, that troubled her also, because she was bound to tell him that although her grandfather was notoriously testy, he'd sat through dinner only an hour or two earlier acting very serene, very calm and unconcerned.

Morgan was puzzled and said so. But then, so was Ellie, and when she eventually saw him to the door, and out into the warm, starlit night where they sat on the porch until her father returned with Morgan's car, at least they had something of mutual interest to discuss.

When her father came on to the porch and handed Morgan the keys to his car, thanking him for the use of the vehicle, she asked what he thought. Her father's face, night-shadowed, turned slightly annoyed.

"We talked a little about that when I got him home, tonight. In fact I had to go in and have a sherry nightcap with him, and he brought it up again. He'd always been able to express himself better with just men around."

Ellie could believe that, but she felt it probably also applied to her father. In fact she wasn't so sure it didn't apply to *all* men, which was proof that she was growing up, that she was learning.

"He's going down to have a talk with Carleton in the morning," said her father. Then he scowled and looked out across the shadowy yard. "The odd thing is that he seems to half believe he *does* need looking after."

Morgan said nothing but Ellie, reading the look of concern on her father's face correctly, said, "That's ridiculous."

Her father looked at her. "Maybe. He told me over the sherry that he was getting tired and old and forgetful. He said perhaps that it didn't really show very much yet. He also said maybe people were just being kind, too."

Sadness touched Ellie's awareness so that even though she continued to defend Grandfather Morris, there was less fire to the words than before. "Dad, even Morgan says his mind is dagger-sharp."

Her father gently inclined his head. "I told him that. I said as far as I was concerned he hadn't changed in twenty years." Her father then straightened up, smiled a little and said, "Don't keep Morgan up late, Ellie. He's got the Morris & Morris job to complete within the next day or two, then he's got to begin on another installation. Good-night, you two."

After her father was gone she turned. "You didn't say anything about the new jobs."

His answer was laconic. "Not much point, duck. Like Caesar said, or should have said at any rate, when you've conquered one world, all the others are just routine." He rose, smiling. "The coffee was good, the company delicious . . . or should that be the other way around?" He reached for her hands, drew her up and stood gazing down into her lifted face for a moment, then he sighed and turned to take her with him out to the parked car.

Summer was over all New England, the night was pleasant, still, awash with stars and a late-rising little sickle-moon. Most of the neighbourhood houses were dark, street-lamps glowed softly, very little sound came from uptown, but then it wouldn't in any case because Windsor was an early-to-bed-early-to-rise town, which meant it hadn't quite abandoned all its old Puritan characteristics.

She said something that had occurred to her earlier — on the drive from the hospital to the Larimore Building, in fact. "Morgan, you've never told me anything about yourself."

He released her hands and leaned on the car. "There's not much to tell. Middle-class background, three years armed service, college. You know the story; it's the tale of two-thirds of all college people. The most exciting thing I've ever done was evolve this Jarrett System. I've never had anything engross me so much." He paused after that, grinned crookedly and said, "Well, there *has* been something that engrossed me more."

He bent suddenly, touched her lips with his mouth then straightened back. It was so sudden, so swift, she scarcely felt it. Then he turned, got into the car and said, "Good-night, Ellie. I'll call you tomorrow."

She nodded, still thrown off by the kiss, and as he backed from the driveway she waved. He waved back.

She returned to the porch, sat, and felt no more tired than as if it were the beginning of a day, not the tag-end of one, although three hours earlier she'd felt tired to the marrow.

She could think back to the first time Arthur had kissed her; it had left her spent, almost listless and breathless. Arthur was very competent in the lovemaking field, too; of course she'd come to realize that his kisses, heady though they invariably were, were part of an act, part of his driving compulsion to prove himself superior, part of the curse that drove him to endlessly excel as an actor.

That kind of a man could kiss perfectly, but it had less actual meaning that the lick of a puppy or the buss of an old grandfather. It certainly had far less sincerity than the kind of little light kiss of genuine affection Morgan had given her.

Morgan's kiss meant affection, understanding, friendship, all the things that a kiss should mean, rather than just desire, or, less intoxicating, play-acting.

She relaxed in the chair and closed her eyes, her lips softly lifted in a tender way. Morgan was so terribly different from Arthur, so honest and sincere.

A chill made her open both eyes. She'd fallen asleep. Her watch said it was two o'clock in the morning! She'd slept more than two and a half hours!

When she rose her legs were cramped and the cold made each joint stiff. She tiptoed inside, reached her bedroom, undressed in darkness, slid between the sheets and sank down into fresh slumber within moments.

She arrived in the kitchen the next morning long after her father had breakfasted and departed. Alice said it was going to be a splendid day for gardening, which was probably a hint, and after Ellie had finished eating she felt alive again. She hadn't actually got very much rest the night before although she'd had something like five hours' sleep.

When they finished the dishes and went out back into the garden her mother said, "Carleton called. He couldn't get anyone to attend his family conference last night. I think he and Michael had words, too. Carleton didn't say as much but I got that impression from some of his remarks."

Ellie related the details of the meeting between Michael and Morgan in the bar-room the day before. Her mother was pleased that they'd patched up their dispute. She then said, "I'm afraid Carleton will just have to forget this incompetency business."

Ellie, recalling what her father had said last night on the porch, debated with herself whether to tell her mother. In the end she decided not to; it could just have been that Grandfather Morris was overly tired last night, or perhaps made unnecessarily mellow by the sherry. But of one thing she began to be suspicious and that was the old man's seeming detachment when he'd been challenged within the family.

She worked in the garden and even carried on a pleasant little conversation with her mother, but her private thoughts were elsewhere most of the time. By noon, when they returned to the house for lunch, she was convinced that Grandfather Morris was up to something. She was also convinced that, insidiously and unspectacularly, she'd fallen in love with Morgan Harding.

The two were hardly related, even in the wildest sense. On the other hand, related or not, they were a fairly weighty pair of decisions to have been arrived at in one morning for someone not yet twenty years old.

Alice had shopping to do in the afternoon and Ellie decided to keep her promise and go and visit Jane Forrest. Her mother left first, brisk and efficient, which she'd have to be after so many decades of marketing. Ellie departed some ten minutes later.

She drove past The Purple Happening café, saw a swarm of people inside eating, thought she would never enter the place again, and when she reached the Forrest residence she had a puckish little sensation of being terribly old and worldly.

Jane was in her bedroom fully dressed but lounging. As at the hospital, the place smelled like a florist's establishment and had the same funereal appearance the hospital room had also had. Jane made a face about the flowers. "You'd think people thought I lived on honey or something. Also, I'm beginning to resent all this solicitation."

"You're an ingrate," said Ellie, handing over the box of chocolates she'd brought along.

"I'm a reject," said Janie, brightening at the

prospect of candy. "Thanks awfully, Ellie. Now I can drown my grief in chocolates. I never cared much for booze, it tastes terrible and makes bubbles go up into my nose. When I drink I sneeze, and that's not very romantic, is it?"

They laughed and talked, and once, when Ellie was gazing out the second-storey window, Jane made a covert study of her profile, then said, "How long does it take a woman to fall out of love, and fall back into love again?"

Ellie turned, brows raised. "Do you consider me an authority?"

"Yes. And I've met him, too. Interesting thing about Windsor: You may *think* people don't see his car outside your house, but they do. Another interesting thing is female intuition. I think I guessed there was *rapport* between you two even before Arthur left. At least I saw it on *his* side, that first time we met, at The Purple Happening."

Ellie, not exactly piqued by all this analysing, none-the-less preferred another topic, so she said, "I just drove by that café. It seemed so — immature, or something — Janie."

The dark girl popped a chocolate into her mouth and offered the box. "Just the thought of the place makes me retch a little, inside. Have a candy and we'll grow fat together."

Janie, obviously, was completely recovered from her broken heart as well as from her near thing with the sleeping pills. By the time Ellie left, she'd got a promise that Janie would drive over to the Jarrett house within a few days, and as she cruised back through town in the fragrant and radiant golden sunlight, she reflected how little impression Arthur had actually made. He'd been gone only a couple of days, and already life was beginning to ignore him as it moved along towards other things, other problems, other solutions.

That, she felt sure, would have been the cruellest blow to Arthur's overwhelming ego she could imagine him ever having to face.

CHAPTER TWENTY-ONE

GRANDFATHER MORRIS SPEAKS

Morgan called shortly before suppertime to ask if she'd care to be his guest at dinner. She declined — because, as she told him, he sounded more in need of rest than her company. He laughed, admitted he was dead-tired, and when she and her mother were in the kitchen a little later, she said it appeared that *someone* was working Morgan much too hard.

The someone, of course, was her father. But when he arrived home somewhat later and both his womenfolk cornered him about this, he denied it, and explained that if Morgan chose to work himself like a robot, there really wasn't too much his employer could do. Then he grinned and excused himself to go get ready for dinner.

The next day Ellie had to go uptown. Her mother, with no such need, was in the rear garden when her husband called to say the family had been invited to Grandfather Morris's mansion that evening for a buffet supper.

"As usual," groused George, "he gives us only one day's notice."

Alice was her placating best. "We weren't going any place, George, and after all these years you ought to be used to Father's idiosyncrasies."

"I'm used to them," shot back her husband. "And I'm also used to death and taxes, but that doesn't make me *like* 'em!"

When Ellie arrived home at midday her mother suggested a later luncheon so they wouldn't be starving by the time they got fed over at Grandfather Morris's place.

Ellie was curious. "What is the occasion, and unless it's something he's just come up with today, I wonder why he didn't tell us over here last night?"

Alice said, "Your grandfather does things his own way, child," and Ellie couldn't possibly have had an argument with that.

When Morgan called in mid-afternoon to jokingly say he was completely rested; in fact was going to take the rest of the day off, now that he'd completed organising and establishing the Jarrett System at Morris & Morris, and asked if she wouldn't like to go driving with him, she had to beg off and tell him why.

"Early dinner at Grandfather Morris's tonight."

His reply was prompt. "You're avoiding me."

"Morgan, that's not true."

"Last night, and now this afternoon."

"I just explained about this afternoon. No matter where we went, I couldn't get back in time to be ready for an early engagement at my grandfather's place. Why are you being so obstinate?"

"Then tomorrow night."

"All right," she said a trifle abruptly. "At seven

o'clock. And I'll be waiting."

After that conversation had been terminated Ellie was still slightly annoyed. She thought he'd only been teasing, he seemed to enjoy teasing her, but she did not really know him so well as yet to be certain.

But as a matter of fact it probably did seem that she was avoiding him. She went to her room to begin the process of getting ready for the dinner. While dressing she made up her mind to be more careful in the future in the way she handled him. It probably would have been better if she'd gone out with him the previous night, even though he could have fallen asleep in her lap; it was his initiative, his plan, and she'd short-circuited it in the manner of a scolding mother.

She told herself that girls had a lot to learn. She also wondered how much time one was allotted for this kind of learning?

Her father arrived home a little early. Not very much earlier than usual, not more than a half hour in fact, but Ellie heard her mother greet him as though he'd sacrificed an entire half day.

Ellie marvelled. Her mother was not a strong nor particularly resolute person, but she had more tact by accident than most women developed over twenty years of arduous effort towards accomplishment.

They met in the parlour before six. Alice looked quite sophisticated with her severely plain gown of apricot colour and her upswept hair.

Ellie was proud of her, and quite obviously so was her husband. He showed approval for Ellie, too, whose dress fitted a little closer, whose figure was a trifle more generous, and whose smooth, handsome face was framed by the red-auburn darkness of her short, curly hair.

"Seems a shame," Jarrett laughed, "to take such beauties over to Grandfather Morris's place, where they'll have to waste all this beauty on just old men. By the way, I think Carleton and Michael will be there." At his wife's look of mild surprise, he added, "I'm not sure, but after we talked this afternoon, Alice, I had occasion to call your brother, and during the course of the conversation he mentioned something about he and Michael having to go somewhere tonight."

Alice wasn't convinced. "George, that doesn't mean they'll be at father's house."

Nothing more was said on this subject, and when George finally swung into the great curving driveway leading up to Grandfather Morris's house, it appeared that Alice was right; there were no other cars out front. The Jarretts were the only guests, at least thus far.

Grandfather Morris met them personally, led them to his baronial sitting-room, and if George or Alice reflected upon the fact that neither of them had visited this room since the angry eruption something like a month and a half ago, they gave no hint of it.

Grandfather Morris's house-staff, one maid who doubled as cook, and one yard man who was also chauffeur upon the rare occasions when Grandfather Morris did not use taxis, and who otherwise doubled as butler and valet, had prepared an excellent little intimate supper.

There was a fine Rhine wine, low enough in alcoholic content to have both bouquet and flavour, and a beef roast so tender it could be sliced with a fork. Moreover, the old man, far from acting as melancholy as George had last seen him, seemed to sparkle this evening, and that, Ellie reflected, was a bit unusual, too. When Grandfather Morris was not looking, and acting, as stern as an old Calvinist preacher, he was out of character. Tonight, Ellie thought, he was up to something.

But it didn't come out until after supper, when they were all seated near the great fieldstone fireplace where some coals glowed despite a warm summer night, and the old man, who had actually barely touched his food, sat back with the air of someone replete and serene. Then he dropped his bombshell. But not right at first. His initial remarks were perhaps designed to heighten everyone's mood of glowing goodwill.

"Your system, according to Michael, hasn't disrupted either the store or the warehouse," he told George Jarrett. "And granting it's a bit early for a tough judgement, it certainly looks as though it'll be very successful."

George was put entirely off-guard. "The credit goes to young Harding, Mister Morris."

"He certainly is an exemplary young man, I'll

have to admit," agreed Ellie's grandfather. "I wish he were in the business."

Ellie, watching Grandfather Morris, thought she detected a very slight hesitancy before he said "business," and it required no stretch of the imagination to substitute the word "family" at least in her own mind.

She remained silent, speculating on all this. Her mother, too, seemed to be watching Grandfather Morris with latent curiosity.

The old man smiled round at them, then he said, "Well, Carleton and Michael were here earlier in the evening."

That brought Ellie's father up a little straighter in his chair, but he did not interrupt. The old man's thin smile lingered.

"We had a discussion of some importance, at least to the family. Michael opposed Carleton's wish that I at least submit to some kind of family supervision. That was gratifying; I'd never really thought Michael would side with me in a disagreement, but he did."

Now they were all watching Grandfather Morris intently, even Ellie's father, whose suspicions had at last been aroused.

"And John Forrest, who was also present, gave it as his suggestion that a family council would be too clumsy, too restrictive." The thin smile did not waver but the tough old eyes were like wet steel. "Didn't I mention that John was also here? Well, you see, I'm getting forgetful. In any event, the scheme Carleton had in mind was over-ridden. He didn't fight very hard for it anyway; his concern seemed to be over what I did with a hundred and fifty thousand dollars of my money.

"I suppose, thinking as Carleton does, that he was justified. He has a great respect for money; can't stand seeing it spent in what he thinks is a foolish manner. Of course I'm responsible, since I hammered that into him all his life. It's ironic that it should come home to roost, isn't it?"

No one answered. Everyone knew the old man was coming to the point of all this. They also knew he wouldn't be rushed, so they sat silent and waited.

"The upshot of all the talk was that one member of the family should act in the capacity of manager for me. As a matter of fact, that was my suggestion. John Forrest agreed and so did Michael. Carleton did, too, but he wasn't very enthusiastic." Grandfather Morris nodded at Ellie. "You," he said.

Ellie was thunderstruck. "I . . . ? Grandfather, I don't know anything about business, about your affairs."

The protest was ignored as the old man glanced from Ellie to her father, her mother, then back again. "Carleton agreed. So did Michael and John Forrest."

"I can't do it," exclaimed Ellie. "I have no training for anything like —"

"No one has any training for the presidency either, Ellie, nor for flying to the moon — but they *learn*. And you have something that's essential — common sense." Grandfather Morris sat a moment eyeing Ellie, his tough gaze hard and unyielding. "You proved up, child, when something much more compelling than simply money, tested you. I'm referring to that actor. Even Carleton agreed with that. Michael and Mister Forrest agreed. You not only can dream, you can employ your inherited common sense. Together, we'll make out just fine."

Ellie's father started to say something, gazed from his wife to his daughter and closed his lips without speaking.

Alice, too, had mixed feelings; it showed in her anxious expression, but she, too, was quiet, so, for almost a full minute, they sat there adjusting to the old man's bombshell-announcement.

He chuckled, eventually. "I've a confession to make; I've had this in mind ever since I first learned Carleton was upset over how I spent my money. I saw, of course, that I couldn't get you back into the company, George, and in a way I was glad, because you proved capable of making it entirely on your own. But I didn't want the family to drift any further apart. And there's something else as well." The old man looked at the glowing coals a moment. "No, I'm not really slipping — yet. But it will happen one of these days. No one is immortal although I suppose most of us like to think we might be." He looked up again.

"This Morgan Harding is exactly the kind of

blood this family needs. George — Alice — tell me I'm wrong."

Neither of them told him anything. It was obvious what he'd been thinking, and even though they, too, had been hoping, even scheming a little, to have it happen, neither of them would have said so, especially in front of their daughter.

The old man was triumphant. He usually was. With his little smile up again he looked at his grand-daughter. "I'm meddling, of course, child, and that got me into hot water once before, but it's a prerogative of old people. But meddling for your own best interests, although you certainly aren't obliged to believe this, nor even to act upon it. In that regard, I can only hope. As for your new position as personal manager of my estate, Mister Forrest has the papers drawn up for all signatures, and that's about all there is to it."

Ellie, with sufficient time to digest all this, now said, "Grandfather, just answer one question for me."

"Certainly. Ask away."

"Are you absolutely positive this is how you want it?"

"As positive, Ellie, as I've ever been of anything in my entire life. Does that answer you?"

"Yes. But I still don't feel qualified at all."

"Leave that to me. We'll work things out famously." Grandfather Morris leaned, covered one of Ellie's hands with one of his and said, "I need someone, Ellie, and you're my choice. Help me, child?"

She leaned with misty eyes, kissed his old cheek and nodded. She had just learned something: That youth, impatient and intemperate as it always was, couldn't always remain so shallow.

CHAPTER TWENTY-TWO

"BECAUSE THERE ARE NO ISLANDS"

When she told Morgan Harding, the following evening, what had happened at Grandfather Morris's place the night before, he wasn't especially surprised, and he showed no doubts at all of her ability to function as the old man's personal manager.

"It'll be valuable experience, Ellie. You'll learn more in a couple of months with him than you'd ever learn in college."

"But I'm afraid, Morgan. It's not just lack of experience. I'm afraid I'll make wrong decisions."

"Not with your grandfather standing by."

They were at that same old-time roadhouse on the northerly boundaries of town having another superb beef dinner as they talked. For once, he seemed neither rumpled nor harassed. The faint shadows that had been under his eyes were gone, and when she asked what he'd done with the afternoon before, he confessed to having driven up-country a few miles and slept beneath a great oak tree until his stomach awakened him, then he'd returned to town, eaten supper out, and had gone to the theatre, where he once again slept.

"Wildly unnerving afternoon it was, love."

They laughed. She said, "I wish I could say the same."

"Stop worrying," he exclaimed. "You are capable. And if you run into an obstacle your grandfather can't help you with, call me." He grinned. "I probably won't be able to help you with it either, but I'll never let you know that."

He teased her, like he almost invariably did, and near the end of the meal he fished out a page from a newspaper and spread it flat, then handed it over. "From a New York City throwsheet."

The entire page was taken up with a bold-face advertisement for a play, and directly below the name of this drama was Arthur Cartier's name and likeness, along with a beautifully fictionalised list of his credits, both at home and abroad. There were a dozen other names, much very favourable writing, and the address of the theatre was repeated four times on the page.

She knew Morgan was watching as she read the page.

Not that it mattered. She folded the paper, handed it back and said, "Arthur's never been abroad in his life."

He wasn't very perturbed. "That's ballyhoo. The world of the Arthur Cartiers is fake from start to finish; not just the people, the producers, the hangers-on, but the background someone fabricates to glamorise all of it." He smiled across the table. "Haven't you ever wondered at the cheapness of the women, at the instability, drunkenness and degeneracy of the men?"

She had, but not very seriously because Windsor was not a place where people of that kind came often nor lingered long.

But she hoped Arthur's play would be a success. She felt that way because Arthur craved success, homage, adulation, the way a normal human being craved water on a hot day, or a good meal after sundown.

"You look sad," he said.

She rallied. "I wasn't being sad. I was hoping Arthur's production makes him rich and famous. He needs those things much more than you and I even want them."

"Charitable," he murmured, obviously unable to share her feeling. "The only thing I hope is that he never comes back to Windsor. Because if he does, next time it won't be an old man he'll deal with, it'll a young one."

"You sound terribly savage, Morgan. I'm frightened."

He blushed.

Later, when he suggested the movie she demurred on the grounds that he'd been there only the night before. He wasn't reluctant, he said, because he'd slept through the feature showing. Nevertheless, they drove up beyond Windsor towards the moonlighted highlands where he sought a low eminence, eased the car atop it facing southward so they had the lights of the town distantly visible in their sight, and he said it still surprised him each time he saw Windsor from this, or some other place, because he'd never thought of it as sitting in a large glen with New England's forested peaks on all sides, but far off.

She teased him. "And you from Cambridge. I'm disappointed. I thought every New Englander understood that in the beginning our forefathers settled only the fertile valleys, that their towns were primarily for defence and whatever commerce cabin-crafts offered."

He lolled aback on the seat beside her. "Go on, teacher, what else can you enlighten me about."

She did a terribly bold thing. She turned, bent and swiftly touched his mouth with her lips. "How is that for a starter?"

He started to straighten up under the steering-wheel but she put a hand on his shoulder forcing him back down. When he did not slacken she opened the door on her side and got out, then she bent and grinned. "Steady, Mister Harding. I was just paying you back."

He climbed out, stretched, then looked across the top of the car. "That makes us even. But you see I'm a person who happens to believe a little healthy debt is a good thing." He started round the car.

She didn't run although there was ample room for it. When he came close she merely put forth a restraining hand. "Down, boy," she admonished. "I'm too old for wrestling."

He stopped. "Are you too old to entertain a

business proposition?"

"I don't like that word very much."

"Sorry. Let me put it another way: As an estate manager for one of the richest individuals in New England, would you entertain a business suggestion from a young man whose prospects are excellent and whose willingness is above reproach?"

"That's better."

"Well. Would you marry me?"

Her lips lay softly closed, her eyes, puckish only a moment earlier, were dark now and unmoving. "Is there some reason why I should?" she whispered.

"Because I love you. I've told you that before, and granting it motivates *me*, I'm searching about for something that might motivate *you*. That's why I mentioned my good prospects. A girl must think of her security."

"Should she?"

"Well . . . don't they, usually?"

"I don't know what they usually do. I don't even care what they usually do."

"I see. Well. . . ."

"Of course I'll marry you," she said, removing the restraining hand.

He was grinning when he touched her, drew her to him and tenderly kissed her. Even afterwards there remained a twinkle in his eyes, but it wasn't altogether a matter of humour, it had become something else, perhaps the rare variety of feeling that can cherish someone with genuine affection and be slightly amused with them, too.

While she kept her face pressed to his chest she was unaware, but the moment she raised her eyes she said, "You are amused, Morgan?"

He held her off at arms length. "I'm in love. I've been that way for some time. Yesterday when I went up-country . . . well, it wasn't to fall asleep under that tree, it was to compose all the heroic and loverly things I intended to say to you today, you see. But the fact is, I did fall asleep even before I got the oration half composed."

"Well, what was the half you got composed?"

"That's it, love. I've forgot it. All of it."

She smiled. "Not much of a memory."

"I've a good memory," he said quickly. "What threw me off was having you accept my proposal of marriage. It completely stopped me."

"I could retract it."

He held her by the arms. "Try it."

"No," she said, with a little head-wag. "I don't much want to be knocked down the way you did Uncle Michael."

"He's *not* your uncle; he's your cousin."

"And you've threatened Arthur. Morgan, I think you must be part American; you have violent propensities."

He dropped both arms, exasperated with her. "You are deliberately baiting me, Ellie."

She smiled, nodding. "You do it to me all the time. It's turn about."

"Will the children be teases, too?"

"Undoubtedly," she said, and after a moment

she also said, "And there'll be no one named *Heloise!*"

He was agreeable as he felt for her fingers, entwined his hand round them and turned to slow-pace beyond the car where moon-dapple lay like dry water down the far slope of their little knoll.

"It is a pretty dreadful name," he conceded. When she halted and her head shot up, he also said, "Very historic, however, very traditional, even melodious . . . but Ellie is just so perfect for you. It's soft and alluring and definitely female and sexy and —"

"You will tire yourself," she said, looking away to hide the smile as she moved out, tugging at him. "Morgan . . . ? I'm happy. Truly happy." She no longer bantered him, and, taking his cue from that, he let the badinage die in the soft moonlight, slid an arm round her waist, gently eased her inward and this time the kiss was long and sultry and slightly unnerving because she felt his needs, his demands, and although her own passions rose in response, it had never before happened like this even with Arthur, so she was shaken a little, flustered and doubtful.

He continued to hold her close in night shadows. There was a tree, some large rocks, and that blue-black New England sky, but otherwise, without looking outward where the lights of Windsor lay, there was nothing else on earth but the two of them.

Later, when they'd resumed their way, neither

of them said very much until, near the farthest slope where they halted she looked up at him.

"For your information my grandfather wants you in the family. He said so right in front of me."

Morgan laughed. "You can't find fault with judgement like that, can you?"

She didn't respond to his humour. "He was meddling again."

Morgan rolled his eyes, then bent a little and placed a finger beneath her chin to lift her face. "Are we going to have another argument?"

She moved her face from left to right very gently. "No. I've decided that my grandfather is a very wise meddler, a very shrewd and knowledgeable meddler, a meddler whose capacity for being right is uncanny. And there are some other meddlers in my life. My parents. They've never said, but they also wanted me to marry you."

He smiled very broadly again. "You see, this impeccable judgement runs in the family."

She nodded. "All right. Have I demonstrated it, too?" Before he could reply, although she saw the same grin starting so she could guess the nature of whatever his answer would have been, she also said, "Never mind. I'm already blinded by the brilliance of your skill as a successful business man, love. I'd rather not risk total blindness by discovering you are an unqualified genius."

He touched her mouth with his lips and hung there to do it again and again. "If everyone is so dead set on seeing us married, maybe we hadn't ought to put it off too long." Their lips touched again, lingeringly this time, then he said, "When . . . ?"

She melted against him. "Any time, Morgan. Have I told you that I love you?"

He held her until she gasped for breath, then gently released her. They turned back towards the car without a sound anywhere nearby. Upon reaching the car he helped her to sit sideways upon the front seat, and leaned upon the open door admiring her.

"You really are breathtakingly lovely. The first time I saw you I couldn't move my eyes."

She remembered. She also remembered the way Arthur had been so upset.

"The night we quarrelled," he went on. "The reason I was so angry was because it made me curl up inside, thinking of you being duped by Cartier. You deserved so much better than he'd ever give you."

She smiled. "You're sweet." Then she swung her legs into the car, tugged the door closed gently and wrinkled her nose at him. "But you look awful when you're angry, Morgan. You really should never be angry in public."

He got under the wheel, sat briefly with both hands atop the wheel, gazing down where Windsor lay in its dark and slumbering big open place, and said, "I remember reading once that every man should be able to look around when he's about to be married, and see everything that will be in his future, even to the cemetery, and if he doesn't like any one small apart of it, he'd better not get married."

Ellie thought that over for a moment and found herself in agreement with it. "Look," she said quietly. "Look down at the town, look at me, look at Jarrett Company in your mind's eye, Morgan...."

He nodded and swung his head. "I don't see a thing I don't like. Not even the smallest thing."

Her head fell to his shoulder as he started the car, eased out the clutch-pedal and let the car go slowly, reluctantly, back down the slope towards the main roadway.

They rode in soft-sad silence almost the full distance back to the Jarrett residence, and there, seeing that lights still burned in the parlour, she straightened up, reached for the door handle and said, "Come along; this'll be the first serious thing we'll have to tell anyone, together."

He joined her on the sidewalk, they kissed then turned resolutely towards her parents' house. Arthur Cartier had never been further from Ellie's thoughts. She couldn't even recall the heartache. It was as though neither had ever existed for her at all.

The employees of G.K. Hall hope you have enjoyed this Large Print book. All our Large Print titles are designed for easy reading, and all our books are made to last. Other G.K. Hall books are available at your library, through selected bookstores, or directly from us.

For information about titles, please call:

(800) 257-5157

To share your comments, please write:

Publisher
G.K. Hall & Co.
P.O. Box 159
Thorndike, ME 04986